Deckart Waldorf knows he's not supposed to be swimming there, but he needs to get away. Sneaking onto the private beach seems like a good idea. His ex would never think to look for him there. After all, Deckart has always followed the letter of the law, in every area of his life. He's never even had a parking ticket.

While snorkeling, Deckart spots what looks like the largest sea snail he's ever seen. He figures it has to be almost five feet in diameter. Unable to help himself, he takes a closer look. Deckart swims around it and even touches the animal. After a few minutes, the beast reaches out to him, revealing tentacles that help it move swiftly, telling him it isn't a snail.

Deckart has no idea what it is, but it doesn't seem dangerous, joining him in playful acrobatics. When he tires and heads to shore, it follows . . . and turns into a man . . . a huge light-browned skinned man named Rawlins who claims they're mates. Can Deckart come to grips with Rawlins's nature before his ex tracks him down again?

Acrobatics with an Ammonite
Copyright © 2022 Charlie Richards
ISBN: 978-1-4874-3538-7
Cover art by Angela Waters

Published by eXtasy Books Inc

Look for us online at:
www.eXtasybooks.com

Acrobatics with an Ammonite Beneath Aquatica's Waves: Book Twelve

By

Charlie Richards

DEDICATION

To all those who've overcome that fear of the unknown in order to take that leap of faith . . . to leap before they looked.

CHAPTER ONE

Turning his *Vespa* onto the gravel road, Deckart Waldorf stopped before a locked gate. He peered around, including checking the road he'd just turned off of, searching for anyone. Finding himself alone, he took a slow deep breath, girding up his courage.

Then Deckart hit the throttle and eased to the left. As quickly as he could, he squeezed his scooter between the end of the gate and a large stone. He knew it was used to keep out trespassers—which was exactly what he was doing—trespassing.

Sweat broke out on Deckart's skin as he returned his bike to the gravel on the other side of the gate. Once again, he paused to glance around the area. Still finding himself alone, he swallowed hard as he began to trundle forward.

It's only for a few days. No one will think to look for me here, least of all my ex.

Deckart's right wrist and arm still ached from his last run-in with Bart Louis. His ex-boyfriend had cornered him in the stairwell of the building where he worked. He'd grabbed his wrist in a hard grip, demanding to know why Deckart had broken up with him . . . via phone.

As if that had been hard to work out.

Deckart felt certain the steroids Bart had to be using to pump up his muscles for body-building competitions—although he'd denied ever touching the stuff when Deckart had asked, which was how their troubles had begun—must have addled his brain.

1

While Deckart had managed to yank his wrist away, earning a few scratches from Bart's nails in the process, his ex had been too fast. He'd grabbed him again, squeezing his upper arm in a hold that was sure to bruise. Only the thud of the door on the landing above them and the appearance of Deckart's boss had saved him.

Fortunately, Renaldo Martinez had taken one look at the situation and had figured out what was going on. "Ah, there you are, Deckart," the man had stated. "Good. We need to hurry to get to the meeting on time."

Bart had been forced to let Deckart leave with his boss. Renaldo had taken him to lunch, even though Deckart had just been returning from his break. His boss had asked if Deckart wanted to press charges, but he'd declined. After all, Bart hadn't actually done anything.

And I don't want him to get the chance, thus, hiding out for a while in order to find a new job.

Renaldo had agreed to the short leave of absence, and he'd assured Deckart that he would give him a glowing review.

That had led to Deckart's decision to camp on a private beach . . . one with a locked gate offering seclusion. It was owned by *World of Aquatica* — a massive marine park a couple of miles to the south. He would have internet access and time away from everyone, allowing him to find a new job in another state.

Somewhere far away from Bart.

Plus, Deckart was a straight-shooter in every aspect of his life. He'd never even had a parking ticket. There was no way Bart would think to look for him trespassing on private property.

No matter how uncomfortable this makes me.

Deckart slowly drove down the gravel lane, keeping his eye out for anyone. While he had a story thought up if anyone caught him, he didn't want to have to use it. Instead, he just wanted to get to the little secluded area he'd spotted on google maps—a little sandy beach with a cluster of trees for shelter, tucked between rocks and out of the weather.

Reaching the bottom of the gravel road, Deckart peered around quickly. He blew out a breath in relief when he didn't spot anyone. Deckart pointed his *Vespa* toward the right, but the second his front tire hit the dry sand, he tilted.

Grimacing, Deckart stepped off his scooter. He righted his vehicle and began to push. By the time he made it fifty yards along the beach, Deckart was already panting heavily and sweat was dripping down his back. Groaning, he kept on pushing.

Deckart spotted the curve of rock and did his best to pick up the pace. He knew from a bit of research that the area he walked along would threaten to be covered at high tide. His timing had been so important to him.

Finally, the rocks gave way to a sprawling beach almost fifty yards across and thirty yards deep. At the top were trees for a number of feet before once again giving way to rocks. He heard birds chirping and insects buzzing.

Grinning, Deckart thought it was perfect.

With a few more grunts and plenty of spilled sweat, Deckart managed to push his *Vespa* amidst the trees. He un-bunjeed his couple of duffle bags and placed them on the ground. From the larger, he pulled out a small, single-person tent. Once he'd finished putting it up amidst the trees, Deckart cast about for stones to make a fire pit. After that was done, he reached his arms over his head and stretched.

The warm afternoon sun heated his already slicked skin, and the lapping of the waves drew his attention.

"Time for a swim," Deckart mumbled. "God, that sounds good."

With a grin, Deckart tugged his polo shirt over his head before draping it over a tree branch. Then he fished through the larger duffle again and pulled out a towel, which he spread on the beach for later. Finally, he tugged free a snorkel, mask, and flippers. Deckart set them aside before pulling out a harpoon gun, too. After a few seconds, he rested that against his scooter for later.

Deciding that, since his shorts were already filthy, Deckart skipped changing them. He toed off his hiking boots before yanking off his socks. Quickly, he donned his flippers, picked up the mask and snorkel, and headed for the oh-so-inviting water.

Deckart hissed when the surf first splashed over his feet and ankles. Pressing on, he strode forward, awkward in his flippers. Still, Deckart kept moving. He could cool off while checking out the fish movements. While he could live on the box of energy bars and bags of dried fruits and nuts he'd brought, he would prefer not to. Exploring for a while would help with that.

Moving quickly, Deckart hoped it helped him warm up. He moved deeper into the water. His skin goose bumped with the chill of the ocean water, but he ignored it.

Once Deckart reached waist-deep, he dunked his goggles in the water, rinsing them. He spat on the lenses on both sides, coating them, then dunked them again. Finally, Deckart fitted them to his face and slipped the snorkel mouthpiece between his lips.

Deckart dove forward and started to swim. He remained on top of the water, putting his face in the waves, breathing through the tube. Roving his gaze over the area, Deckart took in the sandy bottom and the smooth rocks.

As Deckart swam, he searched for good locations where fish would be clustered. He spotted a trench off to his right with a rocky overhang and headed in that direction. Immediately, Deckart noticed several species of fish, crustaceans, and other sea life.

His stomach rumbled, and he suddenly felt sorry he'd left

his spear gun behind.

Then a large shadow to the left caught his eye. He headed in that direction, squinting through the gloom. His heartrate shot up, and he barely resisted gasping when he realized he had to be looking at the largest sea snail he'd ever seen.

The creature had a large, circular shell that had to be nearly five feet in diameter. As he drew closer, he began to circle it and guessed the shell was at least two feet in width. Curiosity getting the better of him, he took a deep breath and dove under the water.

Deckart swam toward the snail slowly. While he'd never heard of an aggressive snail, it was still an animal, and he afforded it the respect it was due. His brows shot up behind his mask as he took in the gorgeous swirls of color in vibrant greens, yellows, and blues on its shell, illuminated by the sunlight filtering through the water.

While Deckart knew it was stupid, he couldn't resist reaching out and touching. The shell slid smoothly under his fingertips. Within the grooves of the swirls, he noted tiny bumps that caught on his skin.

The snail didn't move.

Grinning behind his mask, Deckart placed his palms on the top of the snail's shell and pushed. He floated toward the surface, rotating in a forward roll in the process. When Deckart broke the surface, he took in a deep lungful of air.

Deckart peered under the waves once more and noticed the snail still hadn't moved. Still curious, he dove once again and swam to the snail. He'd just never seen one so big, and he wished he had his underwater camera.

Oops. Left it at home.

Swimming around the snail once more, Deckart slid his palm along the shell as he swam around it.

To Deckart's shock, something began to slither from the base of the shell . . . somethings that appeared to be . . . tentacles.

Okay. Not a snail.

Treading water, Deckart stared in disbelief as one of the tentacles reached toward him and wrapped around his wrist.

Rawlins didn't recognize the human swimming around him. The guy certainly shouldn't have been there. He had every intention of staying perfectly still and allowing him to move on. Then Rawlins planned to report him to security.

Except, Rawlins noticed the scratches and bruising around his right wrist, and for some reason, his interest piqued. He eased a few tentacles out of his shell and stretched them through the water toward the man.

To Rawlins's surprise, the human didn't swim away. He allowed Rawlins to gently wrap two tentacles over the marks, covering them. The water must have softened one of the scabs, for fresh blood lingered within, and Rawlins tasted it through his suction cups.

The sweetly iron-tinged flavor burst across his senses, causing his heart to race and his blood to heat.

Well, holy fucking hell.

Unable to help himself, Rawlins suckled ever-so-lightly on the human's arm, taking in more of the man's life-giving fluid.

So good.

Gods, this human is my mate!

Never in a million years would Rawlins have thought that his mate would just swim right up to him. Yet, there he was. He was with him, doing acrobatics around him.

Considering the bruising, Fate had to have brought the human there to him for a reason. That meant he needed to figure out how to connect.

When the man started to pull at his wrist, drawing Rawlins's attention, his first instinct was to tighten his hold.

Then he saw the way the human was glancing toward the surface and kicking.

Right. Human. Needs air.

Relaxing his grip, Rawlins released his mate. He watched him kick his legs and swish his flippers, rising to the surface. Recalling the way his human had flipped off of him and twirled around him, Rawlins thought about what he could do in his animal state.

Rawlins spread the remainder of his ten tentacles. He had four for feeding—two of which he'd wrapped around the human to taste him—and six for movement. To keep from scaring his mate, Rawlins kept as much of his body inside his shell, peeking his head out just a bit so he could see.

While curling his feeding tentacles close to his shell, Rawlins spread his tentacles used for movement and pushed off the sea floor. He swished his tentacles and closed the distance between them. Nearing the human, he adjusted the way he angled his tentacles and started to rotate in the water, making his shell twirl beneath the waves.

When Rawlins slowed, he refocused on his human. He watched as the guy smiled around his mouthpiece. Rawlins even felt the vibrations of the guy's laughter dance across the skins of his tentacles.

The human took a deep breath and sank beneath the waves. With a few swishes of his arm, he lowered to Rawlins's level. His smile could even be seen around the snorkel's mouthpiece right before he twirled in the water.

If Rawlins could have chuckled while in ammonite form, he would have. Instead, he swished forward a little and bumped his mate lightly with his shell. Then he backed up, and with an undulation of his tentacles, Rawlins made a slow forward roll rotation.

In truth, it wasn't easy in ammonite form. His body wasn't made for water acrobatics. To please and connect with his mate, however, he gave it his best shot.

7

Rawlins wasn't certain how long they continued trading somersaults. He did notice his human's movements slowing, so when the man smoothed his palm over his shell before turning toward shore, he wasn't surprised. As Rawlins watched his mate retreat, he struggled with what to do.

To follow at a distance or shift?

Rawlins did the former first, following his retreating mate. The farther the human moved away from him, the more his desire to shift and be with him grew. It also didn't escape his notice that the human turned and looked at him several times. His curiosity seemed evident.

Deciding to go with his gut, Rawlins began to shift. His ammonite relinquished control easily, allowing his body to flow from sea creature to man. Due to changing from a type of mollusk to a vertebrate, he knew his shift took a little longer than others. From comments made by a few of his friends, Rawlins was also aware that it looked . . . grotesque.

Unfortunately, there wasn't a damn thing he could do about it.

Over the sound of rushing blood and cracking of his shell to form his bones, Rawlins heard his human's shout — the sound one of obvious shock and alarm.

Rawlins pushed harder, changing shape faster than he could ever remember. As his limbs finished forming, he opened his eyes and peered through the ocean. He spotted his human's legs as he rushed toward the shore.

Even though it had been expected, Rawlins still felt a stab of sadness. He hadn't wanted his mate to run from him. Needing to fix it, he got his feet under him and started after him.

With his large, six-foot-five frame, Rawlins quickly broke the surface. He took in a deep breath as he peered in the human's direction. Even though he was fleeing, Rawlins admired the long lines of his back and the smooth, lightly tanned flesh.

Rawlins began closing the distance between them, noticing

the beginnings of a camp at the edge of the woods in the little cove. The place would be inaccessible during high tide. If his mate was hiding from whoever had left those bruises, he'd picked a good place to do it.

Once Rawlins was on the beach and no longer splashing through the water, he realized what the guy was chanting.

"This is not happening. This is not happening."

Shaking his head, Rawlins called, "This *is* happening, my mate. Don't run from me."

Maybe it was the fact that Rawlins had spoken, but his human squeaked and spun to face him. He stared at him with wide blue eyes full of fear that sent a shaft of sadness through Rawlins's gut. His mate's full lips opened and closed, but no words came out.

Lifting his hands in placation, Rawlins continued forward, one slow step at a time. "I didn't mean to frighten you, but didn't I prove that I wouldn't hurt you when we played together beneath the waves?"

Rawlins stopped ten feet in front of his mate when he saw the guy take a step backward.

"You're my fated soul mate," Rawlins declared softly. "Someone I've been waiting for for a very long time. Will you tell me your name?"

For several heartbeats, his human didn't reply. Then his humans whispered, "Deckart. Deckart Waldorf."

Rawlins smiled. "It's nice to meet you, Deckart." He touched his own chest. "I'm Rawlins."

"R-Rawlins," Deckart murmured, sounding beyond confused. "Okay."

Then Deckart's eyes rolled back in his head, and he began to drop.

Lunging forward, Rawlins swept his mate into his arms and cradled him against his chest.

Okay. Now what?

CHAPTER TWO

Floating to consciousness, Deckart realized he felt warm and comfortable . . . and there were thick arms wrapped around his body. The hold was gentle, the man lending him heat, countering his wet shorts.

Deckart struggled to process what exactly had happened. How had he ended up in the arms of . . . whoever? He'd been swimming, playing with an odd sea creature, before tiring.

Right. The thingamabob followed me . . . and turned into a man!

Gasping, Deckart jolted forward, snapping his eyelids open. The stranger's hold eased, but his arms didn't disappear entirely. They lay on his towel with the guy's big body pressed along Deckart's backside.

"Easy, Deck," rumbled a deep voice.

Deckart peered over his shoulder and gaped once more. Eyeing the huge man, he tried to find his tongue. It wasn't easy. The man was *hawt!*

The stranger stared at him with warmth in his pale-gray eyes. His expression had an expectant look to it that Deckart didn't understand. His head was bald, and Deckart felt his fingers twitch with a desire to glide his palms over him. His shoulders were broad, and his medium-brown skin gleamed with moisture.

"Wh-Who . . ." Deckart paused and shook his head. "What?" After clearing his throat, he tried again. "What's going on?" Then something else registered about the handsome man cradling him in his arms. "Y-You're naked."

"I am naked," the man confirmed, sounding completely at

ease with that fact. "I'm Rawlins, remember?" He slid his right hand to Deckart's hip, skimming over his skin lightly, while rising to his left arm's elbow. "I was the ammonite you were playing with."

"Ammonite?" Deckart decided to address that first. "I've never heard of it."

"Not surprising," Rawlins replied with a smile. "The regular ammonite animal went extinct with the dinosaurs, but as a shifter species, we figured out how to survive."

Deckart felt as if his heart skipped a beat. There it was again. Rawlins had claimed to have been the creature—ammonite—that he'd been playing with in the ocean.

"I-I-I . . ." Deckart rolled to a sitting position and wrapped his arms around his legs. He frowned at the ocean, although he couldn't say he was actually seeing it. "I don't understand."

Rawlins lifted his right hand and reached for his jaw, causing Deckart to flinch. Grimacing, the big man rumbled, "Oh, Deckart, my mate." Gently, Rawlins cradled Deckart's jaw. "I would never hurt you, and if you tell me who did that"—he glanced meaningfully at Deckart's right arm and the scratches and bruising there—"I'll make certain he never gets near you again."

Equal parts of confusion and hope began to fill Deckart. "Why? Why do you care?"

"Because you are my mate." Rawlins repeated the confounding words. Evidently, he realized that Deckart didn't understand. Rubbing his thumb lightly along Deckart's jaw, Rawlins smiled. "You don't understand. That's okay. I'll explain everything."

"O-Okay," Deckart murmured. Glancing down at Rawlins's exposed groin, he couldn't help but notice how big the guy was—thick and long, even when semi-flaccid. "Um, and why are you, uh, nude?"

11

Deckart had never considered himself a prude—and truth be told, he loved a large man—but sitting with a complete stranger, naked, was unsettling. Of course, part of it was the fact that Deckart found the man attractive. Regardless of the craziness, he couldn't help how his body was responding to him.

Plus, the gentleness Rawlins was exhibiting was going straight to his head—and heart. It had been so long since he'd been handled so nicely. He wondered if he could trust it.

Bart had been gentle in the beginning, too. And this guy is even bigger.

Rawlins rubbed his thumb over Deckart's jaw again, regaining his attention. "You just grew concerned about something, my mate. If it's because I'm nude, try not to worry." Sitting up, Rawlins moved his left hand to Deckart's back and rubbed up and down, obviously attempting to soothe him. "You're completely safe with me. I'd never do anything you don't want." Rawlins's smile turned a little rueful. "I was out swimming as my ammonite when we met, so of course, I'd be naked when I changed to human form." With a wink, Rawlins finished, "And nothing you have here is going to fit me."

Letting out a snicker despite himself, Deckart clapped a hand over his mouth.

"That's a lovely sound," Rawlins rumbled, leaning close. "I'd love to hear it often."

Deckart felt his brows shoot up. "My ex hated it." Wincing, he muttered, "Shouldn't have said that."

"Did your ex do this?" Rawlins kept his left hand on Deckart's back while moving his other hand from his jaw to his arm. "You flinched from me," he pointed out as he gently cradled Deckart's arm, just below his elbow, in one large hand. "So I figure it's not too far of a stretch to guess that he was abusive."

"Yeah," Deckart murmured, seeing no point in hiding the truth. "Bart ended up abusive."

"How long ago did you leave him?" Rawlins brought Deckart's arm up to his lips. His gray eyes held a surprisingly deep amount of affection as he touched his lips to Deckart's scrapes and kissed them lightly. "Couldn't have been that long ago if he's still coming after you," he mumbled before kissing him again.

The move causes goose bumps to break out on Deckart's skin. The hairs on his arm stood on end. His breath even caught in his throat, and his blood heated further.

"H-Holy shit," Deckart muttered, staring at Rawlins. "Why am I reacting like this?"

Rawlins smiled back at him. "Because you are my mate," he claimed once more. "The other half of my soul. Now that I've met you, you're my reason for being." Sliding his hand down to twine his fingers with Deckart's, Rawlins boldly claimed, "I will devote all my considerable resources to making you safe and happy." Waggling his brows, Rawlins added, "And to keeping you extremely satisfied."

Deckart felt his dick twitch as Rawlins's meaning sank in. "Holy shit."

He couldn't think up another response.

Rawlins could smell Deckart's arousal, and it made his mouth water with a desire to taste him. With his mate next to him, wet and half-naked, he couldn't help his body's reaction. His cock thickened, stretching from his groin.

Unfortunately, Rawlins didn't think it was the right time to move onto the carnal side of their soon-to-be relationship, so he did his best to ignore it. He needed to think of his mate's safety. That meant finding out more about the abusive ex.

"As much as I'd prefer to talk about how you respond to me," Rawlins began slowly, lifting Deckart's scraped wrist toward his mouth again. "I need to keep you safe just as much as I need to pleasure you." Licking over the wounds again, Rawlins bathed them in his saliva. Traces of sea salt clung to Deckart's skin, mixing pleasantly with his mate's natural flavor. "Can you tell me a little about him?"

"I-I'd rather talk about my responses to you, too," Deckart whispered, his attention focused on where Rawlins licked him. "Why are you doing that?" Gasping, he snapped his attention to Rawlins's face as his eyes grew wide and his entire body tensed. "Are shifters blood-drinkers? Are you vampires?" Just as quickly, Deckart added, "Oh my god. I can't believe I just asked that."

Rawlins chuckled softly as he wrapped his left arm around Deckart's waist. Using the hold, he scootched his mate close, flushing their sides together. He couldn't help how much he enjoyed the feel of Deckart in his arms.

"No, vampires are different." Rawlins smiled as Deckart continued to stare at him with wide eyes. "And I'm bathing your cuts in my saliva because, as my mate, it'll speed your healing." Knowing that seeing was often believing, Rawlins turned Deckart's wrist so his mate could see where he'd been gently licking and lightly suckling. "See?"

The scratches were damn near almost gone.

"Oh my god," Deckart repeated, seemingly stuck on that. "How?" He frowned. "Wait. You just said." Licking his lips before swallowing so hard his Adam's apple bobbed, Deckart stared up at him. "You're a shifter. You're obviously sentient while you're an animal," he guessed, and Rawlins nodded in confirmation, even though it wasn't a question. "And you believe I'm your soul mate."

Again, Rawlins nodded, so very pleased that Deckart was picking up everything so swiftly.

His next question meant Rawlins hadn't been doing such a great job explaining after all.

Deckart met Rawlins's gaze and asked, "So, what's it mean

to be a mate?"

Rawlins quickly thought over everything he'd said, but he couldn't figure out how much plainer he could be. Still, he tried again. "Because paranormals live longer than humans . . . a shifter can live upward of five hundred years . . . Fate gives us a mate," he began haltingly, deciding to return to the basics. "We search for him or her, and we believe finding him, in this case, you, is a gift. You're the one person I can bond with. Someone who'll complete me, give meaning to my life."

"Wow," Deckart whispered. "Five hundred years?" He swept his gaze over Rawlins's frame again, his focus snagging for a few seconds on his straining erection. After clearing his throat, Deckart lifted his attention back to Rawlins's face. "So, um, is it rude to ask how old you are?"

While that wasn't what Rawlins thought Deckart would ask about, he replied, "I've existed for over two hundred years, walking the earth and swimming in the oceans." Unable to resist, he squeezed his mate's hand and added, "Alone. Searching. And now, Fate has given me the greatest gift. You."

"I-I kind of th-think it's the other way around," Deckart whispered, his smile appearing tentative. "Because that means Fate is giving me you." After nibbling his lip for a second, he continued, "A-And you said you'd never hurt me, right?"

"Correct," Rawlins assured. Releasing Deckart's hand, he lifted it to his face. He teased his fingertips along his jawline and told him, "Like I said, a shifter is hardwired to please their mate . . . in all ways. We would never intentionally hurt them." Grimacing, Rawlins added, "Of course, I've never been in a relationship, having always been waiting for my mate, so I may screw up from time to time." Rawlins pinned a beseeching look on Deckart. "Please, just give me a chance to fix my mistakes. I'd never want you to try to leave me because of them."

Deckart nodded once. "Deal. As long as you promise the same."

Rawlins shook his head, which caused Deckart's brows to draw together. "Shit," he muttered. "Screwing up already. Um, what I mean is, I'll never leave you." Scoffing, Rawlins added, "After we bond, I won't even be able to get it up for anyone else, and we paranormals have a high sex drive, to begin with." He glanced pointedly at his hard prick. "Once we meet our mate, we become even more randy."

He'd noticed it happen with other shifters.

Cocking his head, Deckart asked, "So, this is just about sex? And what's bonding?"

"Bonding is done through sex. I spill my seed in you and bite you, claiming you here, marking you inside and out as my mate. You'll orgasm from it," Rawlins explained quickly, waggling his eyebrows. Not wanting his mate to get the wrong idea, as he touched the fleshy spot where Deckart's neck met his shoulder, he continued, "But this isn't just about sex. It's about companionship. Once we bond, your life will extend to match mine, and we'll be each other's everything for the next coupla hundred plus years." Deciding to throw it out there, Rawlins added, "Living together. Building a relationship. And someday, loving each other. Partners . . . in all things."

Deckart stared at him with eyes that had grown wider and wider the more Rawlins had talked. "Wow," he murmured. "That's . . . uh . . . shifters do things fast." Then his eyebrows furrowed, and he asked, "How do you know that I'm your special fated mate? Couldn't you be wrong?"

Shaking his head, Rawlins assured, "I knew you were mine the second I tasted your blood."

"My blood?" Deckart winced. "Um, gross." Glancing at his

wrist, he frowned. "Um, not that I don't appreciate it."

Rawlins chuckled as he shook his head again. "You misunderstand." Upon seeing the confusion enter his mate's gorgeous blue eyes, he told him, "Most shifters recognize their mate by scent, but we were underwater when we met. Still, something drew me to you." Humming, Rawlins smiled, revealing, "When I was in ammonite form, I wrapped one of my feeding tentacles around your wrist, directly over your scrapes. I tasted you then." With a shrug, Rawlins admitted, "If you hadn't been my mate, I wouldn't have engaged you. I would have waited until you left, swam home, and reported you to our pod enforcer." Rawlins winced, admitting, "An enforcer, uh, you would have thought him security, would have come to see what you were doing here." Scoffing, he added, "Of course, once he or she realized you were hiding from an abusive ex, my pod still would have helped you escape him." With a wink, he stated, "There just wouldn't have been the epic paranormal reveal and the upcoming mind-blowing sex."

Once again, by the time Rawlins finished talking, Deckart gaped at him. He gently crooked his forefingers and used them to close his mate's mouth. Then he paused, unable to draw his gaze away from Deckart's plump, enticing lips.

"May I kiss you?" Rawlins asked. "Please say yes."

He would have been embarrassed by the deep timbre of his voice, how it betrayed his need, but damn, this was his mate. He'd waited so long for this one small human. He wanted to taste him properly more than he wanted his next breath.

"Is this all really happening?" Deckart murmured, sweeping his gaze over Rawlins's face searchingly. "I'm not in a coma in the hospital because Bart beat me up or asleep in my bed, dreaming of a way out of my crappy relationship?"

Growling softly, Rawlins shook his head once. "Neither of those things. This is real."

"Good," Deckart whispered, reaching for him. As he wrapped his arms around Rawlins, he stated, "Because if I wake up, and this all turns out to be in my head, I'll be really pissed."

Chuckling huskily, Rawlins reveled in the first tentative touches of his mate as he wrapped them around his shoulders. "Oh, my mate. Not a dream. Not a coma." Then he let out a soft growl and muttered, "And if this Bart asshole comes around, I'll show him what a real beating is."

Deckart shook his head as he tugged and began easing backward. "No. Don't want to see you get hurt."

Rawlins went with the move, more than happy to lie with Deckart. As he sealed his mouth over his mate, he realized there were so many things he still needed to explain about paranormals—like increased speed, heightened senses, and healing. Then Deckart opened his mouth to his questing tongue, accepting him, allowing Rawlins to taste his mate properly for the first time, and all thought of anything but relishing the gorgeous, pliant human in his arms fled his mind.

CHAPTER THREE

Even though Deckart could think of dozens of reasons why he shouldn't be doing this, he knew there were just as many reasons to give in to the man — shifter.

The fact that he kisses like a god is only one of them.

Deckart opened eagerly when Rawlins prodded his lips with his tongue. He welcomed the other man's mobile appendage, teasing along it with his own. Rawlins's flavor seemed to burst across his taste buds, and he moaned at the heady masculine flavor of the man.

Rawlins fed him a moan of his own as he threaded his right hand through Deckart's short hair. He cradled his skull, then used the hold to tip Deckart's head to the side, just a smidge. The move allowed Rawlins to deepen the kiss, and Deckart was only too happy to go along for the ride.

Time seemed to stop as their kiss went on and on. Occasionally, Rawlins would break the kiss, giving them the chance to suck in a much-needed lungful of air. He would then dive back in, starting anew.

Deckart couldn't remember a time when his cock ached so badly, and he shifted restlessly beneath the much-larger man. Digging his fingers into the hard flesh of Rawlins's shoulders, he gripped tightly, feeding the man a moan. He wrapped his right leg around the man's waist and used the leverage to buck up against the guy's slightly pudgy stomach.

To Deckart's pleasure, he felt an answering erection grind along his thigh.

Then Rawlins groaned and lifted his head, breaking the

kiss. Deckart's fear that he'd done something wrong lasted no more than an instant. Rawlins stared at him with feral hunger darkening his eyes to a stormy gray as he hooked Deckart's thigh with his left arm and brought it higher on his waist, locking them together more intimately.

Holding Deckart's gaze, Rawlins lowered his hips as he held his weight on his right arm. He dipped his head and pressed his lips to Deckart's shoulder, sucking and nipping provocatively. Deckart felt his cock throb, and he moaned, wanting more, wanting everything.

Except, he still wore his shorts — *wet* shorts.

Deckart groaned and reached between them. Fortunately, Rawlins must have figured out what he wanted, for he obliged by lifting his hips. Taking advantage, Deckart quickly shoved his shorts down the few inches he could, freeing his cock and balls.

As soon as Deckart pulled his hand from between them, Rawlins was pressing against him again. The heat of his hard flesh against his cooler member caused his body to arch in sensual overload. His balls instantly pulled tight, and he could do nothing to stop it.

Within the next couple of heartbeats, Deckart's orgasm crashed through his body. He jolted and shuddered with each bliss-inducing wave of sensation that cascaded over his senses. Fiery pleasure burned him from the inside out, sending him soaring.

Clutching Rawlins close, Deckart hung on for dear life, fearing he would float away without the man's heavy body pressing him into the towel. Through his haze of pleasure, he felt Rawlins's big body shudder. His hips jerked spastically against Deckart's own, and the heat of burst after burst of seed warmed his belly.

Deckart moaned softly, a new kind of pleasure filling him

upon feeling the big man above him losing himself and marking him. Petting down Rawlins's back, he enjoyed the feel of the smooth skin covering his broad torso. With his arms over the other man's shoulders, he could barely reach halfway down . . . he was that big.

Except, with Rawlins, Deckart felt safe in a way he had never felt with . . . anyone.

Rawlins kept part of his weight off of him, even during the throes of orgasm. On the arm that bore his weight, that hand gently cradled his head, scratching over his scalp pleasantly. His other hand still gripped Deckart's thigh, only to move up his leg to cradle his ass to massage sensuously.

Everything Rawlins did seemed to be geared toward pleasing Deckart . . . whether by just holding him or by blowing his mind with pleasure.

He did say his nature is to take care of me . . . in all ways.

A need to take care of Rawlins, too, coiled in Deckart's gut, and he bussed a kiss to his new lover's jaw. "So," he whispered into the big man's ear. "Does that epic claiming bite have to be given when your cock is in me?" Deckart wanted Rawlins to know he accepted him, every bit of him. "Or can you start our bond now?"

With a groan, Rawlins lifted his head. His eyes were filled with an astonishing mixture of want and concern. He roved his gaze over Deckart's face for a few seconds before he licked his lips.

"I can bite you now, my mate." Then Rawlins warned, "But it can never be undone." His gray eyes seemed to darken to the color of thunderheads. "Once I mark you, I'll never let you go." After another heartbeat, Rawlins added, "This is marriage without the possibility of divorce. It is for eternity."

For just a second, Deckart hesitated. Except, then he remembered everything else Rawlins had shared about shifters and fated mates and bonding. Grinning, he tipped his head to the side, baring his neck in invitation.

When Rawlins still hesitated, Deckart murmured, "And, yet, you will never raise a hand to hurt me, belittle me with words, or step out on me." He held Rawlins's gaze steadily while finishing, "I offer you the same pledge. I want to be yours just as I want you to be mine."

And as odd as it was, Deckart truly felt that way. He wanted this amazing shifter to be his. The man was everything he could hope for in a partner and more.

"You're certain?" Rawlins asked once more.

Deckart nodded. "I'm certain."

Rawlins didn't ask again. Instead, his canines lengthened, revealing a wicked set of eye-teeth. Before Deckart could gasp in surprise at the sight, Rawlins snapped his head forward and buried those teeth into the same flesh he'd been working.

For just an instant, Deckart feared he'd made a horrible mistake. Pain spiked through his shoulder. Except, he didn't even have the chance to cry out before that sensation morphed into the most delicious tingles, and ecstasy erupted in his veins. Deckart's nipples beaded as the sensation swiftly traveled down his chest to center in his balls.

Just as Rawlins had told him, Deckart was quickly blindsided by a second orgasm. Spots danced behind his eyes as his cock shot. Endorphins pulsed through him over and over, sending his senses reeling.

Groaning Rawlins's name, Deckart clung once more. He knew he was digging his nails into his new lover's shoulders, but he couldn't seem to help himself. His body bowed with the pleasure Rawlins induced, and he lost all control.

The feel of Rawlins once more licking his flesh, which created the most delicious of goose bumps to rise on his shoulders, pulled Deckart from where he'd been drifting on endorphins. He hummed and turned his head just a smidge, rubbing his face against Rawlins's. When the shifter lifted his head and smiled down at him, his expression filled with smugness, Deckart smiled back at him.

"Wow." Hearing the slight slur in his voice, Deckart barked a laugh. "Damn."

Rawlins licked his lips and swallowed, traces of red disappearing from them.

Deckart sucked in a sharp gasp, realizing what that was.
My blood.

To Deckart's surprise, he realized he didn't mind. He didn't mind the fact that this shifter had just ingested his blood. Instead, he felt a measure of pride that he'd driven this big, obviously strong, man to such heights of need that he'd given in to some instinct that—while Deckart didn't understand it—he would bet anything that it was as old as time.

Such a heady thing to experience.

"Thank you, Deckart," Rawlins rumbled, before pecking a kiss to his lips. He followed that up by dipping his head and nuzzling his smooth cheek against Deckart's while whispering in his ear, "You have no idea how much you mean to me, but I'll prove it to you in time."

Humming, Deckart nuzzled Rawlins's cheek right back. Hearing the big man's sigh and feeling his hand skimming over his side, he smiled, knowing that he'd pleased his new lover. Deckart managed to unclench his fingers, easing his nails from the other man's shoulders.

Rawlins grunted, then glanced left and right. To Deckart's surprise, when the big man met his gaze again, he grinned broadly. "Damn, baby," he rumbled, pleasure lighting his gray eyes. "I love wearing your marks."

Deckart couldn't help but grin. "Really?"

Nodding, Rawlins told him, "You can mark me any time you want." Then he grimaced as he peered to the right. "But we have visitors now." Scoffing, Rawlins admitted, "I should have expected it, but finding you . . . I got swept up in the moment."

"What do you mean?" Unease slithered through Deckart.

With a shrug and a rueful grin curving his full lips, Rawlins told him, "I forgot that any entrance into this place is monitored."

Gasping, Deckart froze. "Monitored?"

Rawlins nodded. "My people know you're here, and they'll be here . . . now."

To Deckart's utter embarrassment — and more than a bit of jealousy — Rawlins stayed sprawled over him, his nudity on display, and he called over his shoulder, "Which enforcer is dropping by? And be warned, he's my mate."

Wait. Why the warning? Was something wrong with that?

Scenting the sudden spike of fear in Deckart's scent, Rawlins realized that he should have phrased that differently. He immediately focused on his mate and rubbed his fingertips across his scalp. Rawlins even offered him a reassuring smile.

"Relax, my mate," Rawlins crooned, knowing he needed to correct the issue. "I just meant to warn them not to upset you because you're important to me."

Deckart slowly relaxed beneath him as he nodded. "O-Okay. Um." His brows furrowed. "Why?"

"Because shifters are a jealous and overprotective lot."

Rawlins recognized the Scottish brogue of Enforcer Craeg, a minke whale shifter. When several other enforcer shifters had found their mates, he'd been promoted along with a couple of others. From what he'd heard, the male had been a kick-ass tracker, even in human form, and he was hella-reliable.

"Exactly," Rawlins agreed as he refocused on Deckart. Then he turned his head and ordered, "So give us a minute to clean up, and I sure as hell hope one of you have sweatpants in my size."

"Oh, for fucking sake," another voice grumbled. Rawlins knew him as Pisces, a bottle-nosed dolphin shifter and tracker for the pod. "I'll call and have some brought." His voice barely carried over the waves since he wasn't bothering to yell, his annoyance clear. "I get there's no way you're trusting us to escort him while you swim. We'll get it done."

"Exactly," Rawlins replied, not bothering to raise his voice either. Upon seeing Deckart's confused expression, he explained, "Most paranormals have heightened hearing. Pisces was giving me a bit of shit about how I wouldn't trust your care to anyone else for however long it took me to swim back to our underground cavern." Rawlins shrugged. "He was right. I want sweatpants so I can accompany you." Then he furrowed his brows as he glanced left and right. "Although, I could just wear the towel, if that's okay with you."

"Uhhh . . . I'm so confused again," Deckart whispered, clearly not keeping up. "D-Do, uh . . . Do whatever you think."

Pleased with his mate's trust in him, Rawlins pressed a swift hard kiss to his lips before easing backward. Then he called, "Stay where you are for two minutes, guys," he ordered. "I need it, or I'm going to gouge your eyes out of your skulls."

While Rawlins spotted Deckart's surprised expression, he winked at his human and rose to his feet. Holding out his hand, he offered, "Let's head to the ocean for a sec and get cleaned up." Rawlins pointed at the towel and added, "Then you can pull on something more comfortable, and I'll wrap your towel around my waist."

To Rawlins's relief, Deckart nodded. "Okay."

Rawlins led an uncomfortable Deckart to the surf, judging by his scent as well as the way he kept glancing around. To Rawlins's relief, his fellow shifters stayed out of sight around the bend in the rocks while they rinsed. As Deckart pulled on a clean pair of cargo shorts and a pale blue polo shirt that brought out his eyes, Rawlins shook out the towel before wrapping it around his waist.

Deckart was just slipping on his sandals when Craeg and Pisces rounded the rocks, entering the secluded beach. Craeg's shaggy auburn locks waved around his head in the wind as he grinned at them both, his green eyes twinkling. He must not have missed the way Deckart eased closer to Rawlins upon their arrival, most likely due to Craeg's thickly muscled six-foot-three frame, for his smile dimmed just a little.

As Rawlins wrapped his arm around Deckart's waist, he murmured, "Relax, my mate. These are friends." He indicated each man in turn. "Craeg. He's an enforcer for our pod. And that's Pisces. He's one of the best damn trackers there is."

While Deckart nodded, he didn't try to offer his hand, and neither man moved to touch him, either.

Pisces glossed over the moment by saying, "Well, damn, Rawlins. I'm jealous as hell." He crossed his arms over his chest and shook his head even as he grinned, lessening the effect of his words. "I was sure I would be the next one to find my mate. Jealous. As. Hell." Then Pisces winked at Deckart. "Especially since he's a little hottie."

"Get your own mate," Rawlins snapped on reflex, even though in his mind, he knew Pisces was just trying to put Deckart at ease.

Tipping his head back, Pisces laughed. "Believe you me," he quipped back. "I am trying." Then he glanced around and clapped his hands. "Okay. So. Let's dismantle camp, and we'll get you both back to our pod's housing."

Craeg nodded as he headed toward the tent. "Alpha Kaiser is waiting for a report," he told them. His eyes narrowed as he picked up the harpoon gun and returned his attention to Deckart. "Please tell me you're not out here poaching."

Deckart quickly shook his head. "No, never. I have a fishing license with all the extras." Grimacing, he admitted, "I, uh, I was just planning to feed myself while hiding out from my ex and finding a job in another state."

"Another state?" Rawlins felt alarm course through not only himself, but also his animal. "You can't leave now."

Gripping Rawlins's wrist where he had it on Deckart's side, he peered up at him with fear in his blue eyes. Still, he said, "I know, Rawlins. I understand that. I just . . . he asked, and that had been my plan before meeting you." As Deckart rambled, Rawlins's emotions settled. "Bart's shown up at my apartment building, but I wouldn't buzz him in. I know it's just a matter of time until he gets around that. And he's shown up at my work, but my boss happening upon us saved me."

"He the one who did that?" Craeg pointed at the bruises lingering on Deckart's right arm.

Deckart nodded.

Craeg growled and muttered under his breath about assholes as he began breaking down the tent.

Pisces curled his lip in a sneer as the playfulness disappeared from his usually fun-loving visage. "Don't worry, Deck," he assured, a cold bite filling his tone. "We'll take real good care of him if he ever tries anything else."

CHAPTER FOUR

Deckart decided he finally understood how Neo felt when he took the red pill. He'd fallen into an alternate reality. Never in his wildest imaginations would he have believed that shifters were real . . . or vampires or gargoyles.

Except, as the friendly pair helped Deckart pack his stuff and head back to the road, they'd expanded on the information that Rawlins had told him. The world was a much larger place than the average human would ever realize. The biggest thing all three of them had stressed was secrecy. Paranormals stayed safe because the human race at large didn't know about them.

Deckart had instantly agreed, completely understanding. While an individual human was typically smart and rational, a group could quickly fall into a fear-induced tailspin. That normally ended very badly for all parties involved.

Craeg had insisted on pushing his *Vespa* while Pisces had carried his larger, heavier duffle bag. When Rawlins had offered to carry his smaller duffle, he'd hesitated. Seeing his new lover's eager expression had him relinquishing the item.

He was still worried, though, so he warned, "It has my laptop on the bottom, underneath the clothes."

Rawlins seemed to understand, for he replied, "I'll be careful."

Then Rawlins wrapped his other arm around his waist, and they all traipsed across the sand.

Craeg didn't struggle with his scooter at all, and Deckart had to say, "You make that look so easy."

Offering a rakish grin, Craeg replied in his Scottish brogue, "A shifter be a might stronger than the average human, and look at me"—he didn't even pause in pushing the *Vespa* as he lifted one arm to flex his impressive bicep—"I'm stronger than many."

When Deckart mouthed, *wow*, Rawlins growled, "Mine are bigger." Then he flexed, too.

"That they are," Craeg agreed with a relaxed air that spoke of his own self-confidence.

Deckart felt his mouth water upon seeing Rawlins's guns. They were definitely big, almost bodybuilder big. With the way he carried a little extra weight around the middle, Rawlins also appeared to be comfortable with himself enough to enjoy life, too.

Not like Bart, who's on a strict diet and insisted I eat that way, too, whenever I dined with him.

Pushing thoughts of his ex from his mind, Deckart focused on Rawlins. "Your guns are amazing," he murmured appreciatively, sweeping his gaze over his towel-clad form. "All of you is amazing."

"Thank you, baby," Rawlins rumbled, clearly pleased. He squeezed Deckart's hip affectionately. "I think you're pretty spectacular, too."

"Aaand here we go," Pisces stated with a fake-sounding put-upon sigh. "Now we get to listen to them trade compliments all the way back to the condos."

"Not we. You," Craeg countered. He dug a set of keys from his pocket and tossed them at Pisces, who deftly caught them. "I'm driving the *Vespa*. You take 'em."

"Awww, man. Really?"

"Yep," Craeg insisted with a chuckle. "Perks of being the enforcer."

"Fine," Pisces muttered.

"Um, I could just drive it myself," Deckart pointed out. "It *is* mine, after all."

"Nope," Rawlins countered before pecking a kiss to Deckart's temple. "I need you close for now, and there's no way I could fit on that thing." Then Rawlins smirked at Pisces. "You would fit on the back, though, Pisces. I can drive us."

Pisces immediately brightened. "Hey, that's right." He grinned at Craeg. "You mind if I ride bitch, man?"

"Don't you have a motorcycle?" Craeg sounded more than a little confused. "Why do you want to ride this so bad?"

Shrugging, Pisces stated, "Because I never have before."

With a roll of his eyes, Craeg muttered, "Fine."

"Yessss," Pisces hissed, even doing a fist-pump.

Deckart wondered if they always acted that way, or if their antics were for his benefit, to help him relax in their company. Either way, it was working. He found them fun and friendly.

After they'd loaded everything into what ended up being a high-end *BMW* SUV, Pisces handed the keys to Rawlins. To Deckart's surprise, his lover opened the front passenger door for him. He even buckled his seatbelt for him.

Lifting his hand to pause Rawlins's action of closing the door, Deckart commented, "You know that I'm not a girl, right?"

Rawlins chuckled, grinning broadly at him. "Oh, my mate. I know you're not a girl." He waggled his eyebrows as he swept a heated gaze over him, pausing at his crotch. "Definitely not a girl." When Rawlins refocused on Deckart's face, his expression sobered. "My only intention is to treat you as the special gift you are to my life. This is me taking care of you and expressing how much I appreciate you."

Warmth flooded Deckart's chest, and he had to swallow the sudden lump in his throat. "Wow," he murmured. "You're really good at this."

"This?" Rawlins cocked his head in question.

Nodding, Deckart waved a hand between them. "Knowing what to say to make a guy feel special."

"You *are* special," Rawlins replied, cradling his jaw in one huge palm. "The most special person in my life from now until eternity."

Blinking back unexpected tears, Deckart cleared his throat. "I—" He cleared his throat a second time. "I don't know what to say to that." Then he needed to admit, "Most humans don't believe in love at first sight, but I'm sure heading in that direction. It's a little scary."

"Yes, it is," Rawlins agreed, his gray eyes filling with intensity. "But I'm right there with you."

"Good."

Deckart barely managed to whisper the word before Rawlins's lips were against his own. Immediately opening, he welcomed the other man's tongue. He dueled with his own.

Giving in to his desire, Deckart cradled Rawlins's skull, sliding his fingers over it. The smooth, warm skin heated his palms and caused the hairs on his arms to stand on end. Groaning softly at the exquisite sensations, Deckart thought he would never get enough of kissing this man.

"All right, you two." Craeg's deep brogue cut into their moment. "We need to go. Alpha's waiting."

With a groan, Rawlins brought the mind-melting kiss to an end. "Yes, Enforcer Craeg," he muttered before pecking Deckart's lips one more time.

Craeg's chuckle was cut off by Rawlins closing the door.

As Rawlins turned the SUV into the driveway, he reached over and took Deckart's hand. He'd already explained how everyone living in the private condominium and apartment complexes near *World of Aquatica* was either a shifter or affiliated with one. This was one of the few places in the world where marine shifters gathered and could change in a safe environment.

Deckart squeezed Rawlins's hand back before shifting in his seat. Rawlins could scent his mate's nerves, but he couldn't do anything about them. His words of encouragement would only take the man so far.

His mate needed to meet Alpha Kaiser, who could be a very intimidating man when he wanted to be. He was a powerful businessman in the human world. The alpha had connections in both the human world and the paranormal world, and Rawlins appreciated that he was such a fair and understanding alpha.

"After meeting with Alpha Kaiser, we'll head to my apartment," Rawlins told Deckart. "We can shower and relax. Have a meal. Watch TV." Glancing his mate's way as he parked, he added huskily, "Or some other activity, if you wish."

With his mate next to him, Rawlins realized why so many other mated shifters had such a one-track mind. The allure of his special someone was intense. He wanted to touch and explore, to find every hot spot and erogenous zone. He wanted—

And I better stop thinking like that, or I'm going to be meeting my alpha with a hard-on.

"Um, a shower would be nice," Deckart told him, flashing a smile his way. "So, uh, I guess your alpha doesn't care about you being gay?"

Huh. Forgot that could be a concern for some.

"Not at all," Rawlins assured. "In fact, Alpha Kaiser's own mate is a man. So is his brother's mate. That's William Roush," he added, figuring he should explain a little pod hierarchy before the meeting. "He's our beta. Then there's several enforcers, who ensure we all follow pod law, keeping our people safe."

"Kinda like a little mini kingdom right here in California, huh?" Then Deckart's eyes widened, and he snapped his attention to Rawlins. "Oh my god. Roush. Kaiser and William

Roush. Those Roushes?"

"Yes. Those Roushes," Rawlins confirmed, arching one brow as he eyed Deckart curiously. After putting the SUV in *Park*, he asked, "Have you heard of them?"

Deckart nodded, turning his attention to the condos before him. "Yeah," he mumbled, clearly in awe. "I work at an engineering firm, and my company bid on a couple of the projects that the government was going to do south of *World of Aquatica*." Refocusing on Rawlins, Deckart stated, "From what I heard, Kaiser Roush and his brother produced studies from several environmental groups proving the land was a habitat for a number of endangered species, so it couldn't be developed." Frowning, he mused, "There were a number of unhappy people, from what I heard, but the laws to protect the wildlife are there for a reason."

Rawlins hummed as he unbuckled his seatbelt. "Very true." As he opened his door and pulled the keys from the ignition, he commented, "I think I remember that. It was . . . two years back?"

Obviously following his example, Deckart exited the SUV, too. "Yeah. Just over."

"So, you're an engineer." Rawlins strode around the hood, wanting to be near his mate. "Did you ever go out to that site?"

Deckart shook his head. "Oh, no. I'm not an engineer. I just work for an engineering company. Lintel Engineering." When Rawlins grabbed Deckart's hand and threaded their fingers together, he smiled at the move. "I work in the administration department. I do bookkeeping and accounting. Process timesheets. Expense reports. Update the costs that have been accrued to each project on a weekly basis so the project manager knows how much money they have left. That sort of thing."

Rawlins felt his pride in his mate grow. "Damn, babe.

Sounds like you're pretty important there."

To Rawlins's pleasure, he watched his mate's cheeks take on a pinkish hue even as he scented of pleasure.

"I just like working with numbers," Deckart revealed with a dismissive shrug.

Rawlins guided Deckart into the building, opening the door for him in the process. "Well, everyone's job is important. From the kitchen staff to human resources to the CEO. All cogs in a wheel." Rawlins noticed that Craeg and Pisces fell into step behind them.

"I suppose so. So, what do you do here?" Deckart asked in an obvious attempt to change the subject.

"I'm a cleaner," Rawlins shared.

Frowning, Deckart asked, "Like, housekeeping?"

Chuckling from behind them, Pisces caught their attention. When they half-turned, he stated, "Deckart, you're looking at the best damn window cleaner on the place."

"Window cleaning?" Deckart smiled at Rawlins. "Like, with squeegees and soapy water and stuff?"

"Special glass cleaner, actually," Rawlins clarified. "And yeah. Windows amongst other things. Aquariums, vehicles, floors. You name it, and I've probably cleaned it."

"But Pisces is right." Alpha Kaiser's deep voice came from the open doorway they approached. In a black suit and tie with his black hair slicked back from his face, he could have cut an imposing figure . . . if he hadn't had the jacket off, his sleeves rolled halfway up his forearms, and his shoulder resting against the doorframe. The small smile curving his thin lips helped, too. "Rawlins's claim to fame around here is definitely the windows. The glass on our storefronts have never looked so fantastic." Kaiser straightened and held out his right hand. "Hello, Deckart. It's nice to meet you."

Pride filled him upon hearing his alpha praise his abilities, and his animal practically preened in his mind . . . as much as an ammonite could, anyway.

"Nice to meet you, too, sir," Deckart replied, shaking Kaiser's hand. "Uh, th-thank you for not running me off your land." His mate's cheeks darkened a bit as he said, "Even if it's probably because I ended up being Rawlins's mate. I'll do everything I can to make him just as happy as he's already making me."

Kaiser smiled as he stepped back and indicated that they file into the room. "With that attitude, I'm certain we'll have one very happy ammonite shifter on our hands. Please come in." He headed to the sideboard. "Congratulations on starting your bond. Can I get you anything to drink? Water, beer, wine, spirits?" Pausing to peer back at Deckart, Kaiser added, "Juice?"

When Deckart glanced at Rawlins, he smiled at his mate as he answered his alpha. "A bottle of beer wouldn't go amiss."

"Light or dark?" Kaiser replied.

"Dark, please," Rawlins requested.

As Kaiser reached into the refrigerator, Rawlins could practically watch the inner battle in Deckart's eyes. Finally, he seemed to come to a decision and asked, "Do you have any red wine?"

"Of course," Kaiser answered. "That's one of my own mate's favorites. Merlot, Cab, Malbec?"

"Uh, Malbec would be wonderful," Deckart replied, seeming to start to relax as they settled on a love seat together.

Rawlins wondered if Deckart even realized he cuddled into his side. Then his mate straightened and frowned at him.

"Deckart?" Rawlins questioned, concern filling him.

"You're still only wearing a towel," Deckart pointed out, his brows remaining furrowed. "Is that normal around here?"

Several chuckles could be heard around the room as Rawlins admitted, "Yes."

With a smirk, Craeg offered, "Welcome to the shifter

world."

Staring around at them all with wide eyes, Deckart whispered, "Thanks."

CHAPTER FIVE

Deckart still felt as if he were in shock. For a few minutes, it had only been the five of them. Then others had arrived, and Craeg and Pisces had left. Deckart had been introduced to so many people that he worried he wouldn't be able to keep everyone's names straight.

The prevailing theme, however, was how happy everyone had been for not just Rawlins, but for them both. They'd assured Deckart that Rawlins was a fantastic man, and they would be happy together. A time or two, Deckart had wondered when the second shoe would drop.

Surely this is all too good to be true.

Except, it never did.

Of course, Deckart had needed to explain why he'd been hiding on their beach all over again to Alpha Kaiser, but even that had gone better than anticipated. He'd immediately called someone named Ovram and had ordered him to get everything he could on Bart. Then he'd assured Deckart that they would keep him safe.

Now, Deckart and Rawlins were in the elevator heading for the fifth floor of a different building. Rawlins lived there in a spacious one-bedroom apartment. He'd been given the option to buy, but he'd declined, saying he'd wanted to wait until he found his mate.

"And now that I've found you," Rawlins told Deckart, guiding him out of the elevator. "If you don't like the place or want something bigger, we can buy a different place. If you want kids or an office, we can get a two-bedroom or even more." Rawlins grinned at him as he added, "Kaiser even has plots set aside further out of the way if couples want to have more privacy. He'll build a home for us, and we can buy it from him."

"Wow." Deckart knew he'd been saying that a lot lately. "And Kaiser does this for everyone in his, um, pod?" Just as quickly, he asked, "If you're all ammonites, why do you call it a pod?"

Rawlins chuckled softly. "Guess we did forget to explain that, didn't we?" He stopped at a door and unlocked it as he continued, "Yes, Kaiser offers options to each member of his pod. He knows that a happy shifter works harder and is more content, creating peace in the pod." As Rawlins led the way inside, closing the door behind them, he added, "And no, I'm the only ammonite shifter here. Everyone else is . . . something else. Some other marine creature or semi-aquatic creature."

"Huh. Like what?" Deckart asked curiously. "What's out there?"

"There are most creatures you can think of," Rawlins told him, leading him through a clean living room decorated in a minimalistic but warm style. "From seahorses to whales. That's what Craeg shares his psyche with. A minke whale. Native to Scotland, of course," he added with a chuckle. "Kaiser and his brother are both squid. Colossal and giant, respectively. You met the enforcers, Eban, Dare, and Westram. They're a great white shark, giant octopus, and longnosed saw-shark, in that order. Pisces is a bottle-nosed dolphin."

Deckart held up his hand. "Oh, wow. Stop." He put his fingers near his head, expanding them as he made an exploding noise. "You just overloaded me. Mind blown."

Rawlins chuckled huskily. Wrapping his arm around his shoulders, he squeezed lightly. At the same time, he pecked a kiss to his temple.

"It's a lot to take in."

Then Rawlins headed through a bedroom with the biggest bed Deckart had ever seen. Bigger than a California king, even. Considering his lover's size, that made sense. He didn't stop, though, heading through another doorway and flicking a light switch.

Instantly, Deckart gasped.

It had to be the most wonderful bathroom he'd ever seen outside of a home designer show. There was a double sink vanity, the granite a myriad of green shades, which matched the tile on the floor. The chrome handles were a deep rusty color, and the walls were an ocean blue. Not only was there a massive shower with rainfall showerheads, but there was a deep jetted soaking tub.

"I'm in love," Deckart whispered under his breath, already seeing himself in that tub with a glass of wine and a book.

Rawlins barked a laugh, resting a hip against the counter. "Should I leave you to your affair with my bathroom," he teased, reminding Deckart that shifters had exceptional hearing. Waggling his brows, Rawlins added, "Or are you going to share?"

Deckart felt his cheeks heat, but he shrugged anyway. "I love your tub. If you're okay with me moving in" — *god, I can't believe I'm actually thinking about doing this after only knowing him a few hours* — "you'll find me in there often."

"Fair enough." Rawlins smiled adoringly at him. "If the price of you moving in here is finding you naked and wet in that tub several times a week, I will be so very happy to pay it." His smile turned heated. "Especially if you don't mind me climbing in with you on occasion."

Deckart felt his blood heat as he focused on that idea — a wet, naked Rawlins in the tub with him. "Oh, yes, please." He couldn't recall ever hearing his voice so husky, but his prick had gone from semi-hard from just being around Rawlins to being hard as a steel pipe.

Rawlins groaned, cupping himself through the towel, revealing he was just as turned on. "Fuck, Deck," he muttered. "Your scent is driving me nuts." Blowing out a deep breath, Rawlins rumbled, "You wanted a shower. Is that still the plan?"

As much as Deckart wanted to feel his new lover's rod up his ass, he wanted to get clean, too. He had been sweaty from pushing his *Vespa*, then he'd swam in the ocean, and finally, he'd shot his load all over himself with only saltwater to rinse it. His skin felt crusty, making him feel gross.

"Yeah, sorry." Deckart grimaced as he rubbed at his arms. "I really want a shower." Then a thought occurred, and he peered at Rawlins from beneath his eyelashes. "Um, I don't suppose you'd like to join me?"

Other than gym class, Deckart had never showered with another guy before, and he knew this would be completely different.

After all, he wouldn't have to make certain he kept his gaze averted for fear of repercussions.

"Oh, my mate," Rawlins replied, his voice deep and husky. "There is nothing I want more than to soap you up and rinse you off." Before Deckart could urge him to do just that, Rawlins took his fingers between his own and warned, "But if I do that, I won't be stopping with just that. I will clean you, stretch you, and slide my cock into your body. I'll drive us both out of our minds with pleasure, and I *will* claim you." Rawlins held him in a steady gaze as he finished, "And there is no going back from that. Is that something you're ready for?"

Deckart froze for one heartbeat, two. Then he wondered why the hell he was stalling. He wanted this man, and he wanted everything that he was offering him.

"Yes," Deckart answered. "Yes, I want that, and I'm ready."

With a low groan, Rawlins pulled away and turned toward the shower. He reached inside and turned on the water. At the same time, he untied the towel at his waist, allowing it to drop to the floor.

Deckart nearly swallowed his tongue upon seeing the gorgeous view. Even though the man sported softness around his belly and love handles, there was nothing soft about his ass. His butt cheeks were round and tight, and Deckart wanted to touch so badly . . . so he did.

Reaching out, Deckart boldly cupped one cheek and squeezed experimentally. It felt absolutely fantastic in his hand, and a tremble of need worked through him. He couldn't wait to clutch those babies as Rawlins pounded into his body.

Rawlins's low growl pulled Deckart out of his fantasy. Jerking his attention upward, he quickly released the man. He knew plenty of tops that didn't want their ass touched by their partner, and he suddenly worried that Rawlins would be one of them.

Except, when Deckart met Rawlins's hungry gaze, all he saw was approval and pleasure.

"Y-You liked me gripping your ass," Deckart guessed.

Rawlins sucked in a quick breath and swallowed so hard his Adam's apple bobbed. Then, in a rumbly voice filled with desire, he stated, "Deckart, I like it when you touch me anywhere, and you are welcome to my ass anytime."

For an instant, Deckart gaped. "Y-You'd let me top you?"

Nodding sharply, Rawlins replied, "Of course."

Well, that's unexpected. Welcome, but unexpected.

"I'm mostly a bottom," Deckart admitted with a grin. "But I'll take you up on that one day."

Rawlins's grin turned feral. "And I'm mostly a top, but whenever you're ready, baby, my ass is yours." Then his attention drifted down Deckart's body. "Do you like those clothes?"

"Uh, sure," Deckart replied, uncertain why Rawlins would ask.

"Because if you don't undress, I'm about five seconds from tearing them from your body."

Grinning, Deckart rested his hands on his hips. "Oh really?"

"Yes," Rawlins confirmed. "Oh really."

Deckart didn't move.

Rawlins frowned. "What are you doing?"

Smiling innocently, Deckart replied, "Waiting five seconds."

For just an instant, Rawlins's eyes widened. Then he growled softly and did exactly as he'd threatened.

With the tattered remains of his clothes still drifting to the floor, Deckart laughed as his lover tugged him into the shower.

Rawlins loved the sound of Deckart's happy laughter. Still, as he tugged him under the spray, he reminded himself that his mate was human. He needed to temper his strength.

Never did Rawlins want to accidentally hurt his much smaller and weaker lover.

To that end, once Rawlins had Deckart right where he wanted him—namely, naked and under the shower spray with him—he started a gentle, sensual assault. He began at the top, grabbing his soap in lieu of shampoo, seeing as he didn't have any hair himself, and he massaged it into Deckart's short, light-brown hair. Scratching his scalp rhythmically, Rawlins reveled in Deckart's throaty moan coupled with the way he tipped his head back, giving Rawlins complete access. As Rawlins rinsed the soap thoroughly from his hair, he made a mental note to buy shampoo and conditioner.

Rawlins picked up the loofah and the body wash. After

pouring a healthy dollop onto the neon green poof, he closed the lid and set it back on the shelf. He massaged the loofah for a few seconds, working up a nice lather, before placing it on Deckart's neck.

Working down Deckart's back, Rawlins massaged his shoulders to his shoulder blades. He moved the right arm, scrubbing down it. Reaching his human's hand, he washed between each finger, earning a soft snicker from his mate. Grinning, Rawlins moved back upward, lifting his arm to clean his lightly-haired pit.

To Rawlins's surprise, Deckart didn't seem to be ticklish there. He filed that away as he moved to his mate's left arm, all the while wondering if there were other more sensitive spots. Rawlins received an answer when he teased over his lover's hip bones—both sides—and Deckart hissed and shied away a little.

Rawlins smiled, but he kept going, kneeling behind Deckart. His gorgeous ass was right on display before him. As much as he wanted to pry open his cheeks to reveal his hole, then dive in for a taste, Rawlins resisted.

His mate wanted to be clean, and he would oblige him.

To that end, Rawlins eased the loofah into his crack, while keeping it clinical. He rubbed around and under each cheek, then swiped over his hole. Gritting his teeth upon hearing his mate's sensual moan—coupled with how he rested his hands on the wall and arched his back—Rawlins continued down his right leg.

Deckart's whine of dismay nearly did him in. "Getting you clean, my mate," Rawlins rumbled gruffly. "Just like you wanted." Giving in just a little, he gripped his lover's ass and squeezed. "Play in a minute."

Then Rawlins returned to cleaning his mate.

Once Deckart's legs were finished, including between his

toes, Rawlins urged his mate to turn around. The mouth-watering sight of his human's slender erection greeted him. As Rawlins worked on cleansing Deckart's chest, he couldn't help but stare. He guessed his mate's prick to be around seven inches with a respectable girth.

A perfect mouthful.

"H-Hurry," Deckart pleaded as a bead of pre-cum appeared at his slit. It was quickly rinsed away by the water cascading over them.

Not wanting to miss that treat again, Rawlins did as Deckart had bid. He finished with his mate's chest, then gently rubbed the loofah over the man's ball sack before wrapping it around his length. After two swipes, Rawlins couldn't wait anymore.

Opening his mouth, Rawlins leaned forward and enveloped Deckart's cock head. He sucked half of him in before easing off again. His taste buds flared with the delicious flavor of his mate's skin, regardless of the soap. The bead of pre-cum that hit his tongue, containing just a hint of salt, was the icing on the cake.

Rawlins's own cock throbbed, reminding him of how much more he wanted, needed.

Humming happily, Rawlins gripped Deckart's hip and began blowing him in earnest. He sucked him deep, then backed off quickly. He swiped his tongue over Deckart's crown before teasing his frenulum. Over and over, Rawlins worked Deckart's dick.

He enjoyed the steady flow of pre-cum as well as the heady sound of Deckart's grunts and moans of pleasure.

Grabbing the waterproof lube he kept in the shower to jack off, Rawlins poured a healthy amount onto his fingers. Then he returned one hand to his lover's hip while reaching behind him. He felt for his human's hole, finding it with ease that came from centuries of practice.

Rawlins pushed in his middle finger, sinking it as deeply

as he could. The tight pressure on his digit drew a moan from him as he imagined that squeeze on his cock. He knew it would be exquisite, and his cock jerked as if in agreement.

"Oh, god, Raw," Deckart moaned. "More. Oh, please more."

Figuring his mate knew his body, Rawlins obeyed. As he continued to bob on his mate's prick, he eased his finger partway out before adding a second one. His human never clenched or tightened. Instead, he rocked back and forth between Rawlins's ministrations, and he loosened his hold to let him move at will.

It wasn't long before two fingers became three, and three became four. All the while, Deckart's cock leaked like a sieve in his mouth. His pre-cum coated his tongue, and Rawlins groaned his enjoyment.

The ache in Rawlins's balls spurred him forward, and the next time Deckart rocked back onto his fingers, he hit his prostate with more than just the glancing blows he'd been using to stimulate. He rubbed his fingers around the pleasure-giving nub. Just as Rawlins had expected, Deckart went off like a bottle rocket. His scream of enjoyment filled the shower stall, and his cock erupted in his mouth.

Moaning for a new reason—Deckart's seed tasted damn delicious—Rawlins eased back on his mate's prick. He relished his man's flavor, knowing he would never get enough of it, and he would never have to. This human was his . . . forever.

And now, to cement that.

After Deckart stopped spurting, Rawlins gently eased his fingers from his human's gripping heat. He released his lover's spent dick and rose to his feet. The glazed expression on Deckart's face was a thing of beauty, and he planned to put it there often.

Lifting Deckart, Rawlins reveled in the way his mate immediately spread his legs and wrapped them around his hips.

He pressed his human's back against the shower tiles while supporting his ass with one hand. He used his other to guide his throbbing cock to his mate's hole, wiping the remainder of the lube on his dick in the process.

"Ready?" Rawlins asked, his voice deep and gruff with need.

Deckart blinked once, twice, before some of his bliss-drunk expression eased. Then he grinned at Rawlins. "Yes."

That was all the permission Rawlins needed. He pressed his cock to Deckart's prepared hole and pushed. Moving his free hand to his mate's thigh, he rocked forward, sinking in and in and in.

CHAPTER SIX

Deckart had never been stretched so much or felt so full. He relished the mild burn of pain as he watched his lover's massive erection sink deeper and deeper inside him. Breathing through it, he focused on staying relaxed and pliant in his lover's arms.

When Rawlins's probably eleven-inch cock lay fully seated within him, Deckart let out a low moan of accomplishment. He'd done it. He'd taken his shifter's massive tool.

And gods, does it feel good.

"A-Are you okay?"

Hearing the strained growl in Rawlins's voice, Deckart snapped his attention to him. He smiled. "Better than okay," he whispered around his panting breaths. "Please fuck me." Recalling how careful Rawlins had been with him, Deckart added, "I know I'm human, but I'm not fragile."

Rawlins groaned. "You are compared to me," he countered, but he did start moving. "But I'll try to remember that."

His big dick dragged over Deckart's inner muscles, setting them on fire in the best possible of ways. "Oh, yeah," he moaned. "That's the spot." He sighed, then grunted as Rawlins pushed back into him, rubbing over his prostate. Rocking his hips, Deckart tightened his fingers into Rawlins's shoulders as he encouraged, "More!"

Taking him at his word, Rawlins began speeding up his ruts. He pulled out, pushed in, and repeated. Over and over, he sped up his strokes. With his jaw clenched and his eyes narrowed, Rawlins stared at where they joined, his expression one of feral delight.

Deckart reveled in that expression, his lover's open need and desire, showing how much he needed him. The look went straight to his balls, combining with the way Rawlins pegged his prostate over and over. Deckart's head swam with a fresh surge of arousal, and he felt himself drawing closer and closer to the edge at an alarming rate.

"Oh god!" Deckart whined, doing his best to rock into each rut. It felt so primal to be taken bare in the shower. He knew he should have said something before his lover entered him, but he'd been too out of his head with answering desire. "Oh, fuck, never felt it like this. Feels so good."

"Need you to come," Rawlins demanded, pumping into him faster and faster. "Want to feel you come on my cock. Want to feel you clench with your pleasure."

Deckart moaned upon hearing Rawlins's coarse demands. While he hadn't thought he'd been close enough, it felt as if his body was hardwired to obey. His balls began to tighten, and his body flamed with how hard his erection suddenly throbbed.

"Oh . . . oh, Raw," Deckart whined. "So close."

"Do it," Rawlins demanded, pegging his prostate over and over. "Come for me, mate."

Deckart couldn't have stopped it even if he'd wanted to . . . which he didn't. His second orgasm within a few minutes barreled through him. He shouted his pleasure to the walls as he tipped over the edge, spurting over and over again.

Even floating on the bliss of completion, Deckart noticed when Rawlins slammed home and stilled. The unfamiliar sensation of hot seed flooding his chute warmed him from the inside out. A tremble worked through him at the intimacy of it.

Then a bite of pain stabbed through his shoulder. He hissed, then groaned when the sensation morphed into the

most delicious of tingles. They traveled across his torso, causing his nipples to bead. That same heat seemed to envelop his
cock and balls, and he hardened once more. The sucking sensations where Rawlins had bitten him transferred straight to
his cock, as if he were sucking on it instead.

In seconds, Deckart was blindsided by a third orgasm. He
moaned and shuddered in Rawlins's hold, barely able to keep
his coordination enough to keep his legs around his lover's
waist. As he kept coming and coming, his head spun and
black spots danced across his vision. Deckart knew if Rawlins
hadn't been holding him tight against his body, he would
have melted to the floor in a puddle of blissed-out goo.

Eventually, Deckart began to descend from the cloud of endorphins he'd been soaring on. He felt Rawlins petting his jaw
and turned his head to peck a kiss to his palm. Then he peeled
open eyelids he couldn't remember closing in order to stare
blearily up at the big shifter.

"Hey, my mate," Rawlins rumbled, his deep gray eyes soft
with warmth. "You doing okay?"

"Never better," Deckart mumbled. Sliding his hands up
Rawlins's neck seemed to take a great amount of effort, but
he did it, allowing him to glide his palms over Rawlins's
smooth scalp. "Do you shave?"

The corners of Rawlins's lips twitched as he answered,
"No, it's completely natural. I've always been bald."

"Huh." Deckart sighed again, then registered that Rawlins
still had his dick in his chute . . . and he was still mostly hard.
"Shifter stamina," he whispered, gently clenching and releasing on the member invading his ass. "Wow."

Groaning softly, Rawlins nodded. "Yeah. I wanna take you
to bed and go again."

Grinning at Rawlins's blunt statement, Deckart murmured,
"I'd love that." As his lover reached over and turned off the
water, he cleared his throat and asked, "So, uh, I'm clean, but

we sorta forgot to discuss that part before going without a condom."

Rawlins snapped his gaze to him, his lips parting a little in obvious surprise. "Oh, shit," he muttered, shaking his head. "Guess I forgot to explain that bit."

"What bit is that?"

As Rawlins carried Deckart out of the shower without even removing his cock, he shared about paranormal strength, speed, healing, and how they couldn't get or pass on human diseases.

"Very nice," Deckart muttered right before Rawlins fucked him through the mattress.

As was customary for when a shifter found his mate, Alpha Kaiser had given Rawlins a week off to strengthen his bond with his mate. Over the last couple of days, Rawlins had been enjoying every second of it.

Noticing Deckart walking a little stiffly earlier that afternoon, Rawlins had felt a little guilty. He hadn't been able to get enough of his mate's ass, and he knew he wasn't a small man. Even by shifter standards, his eleven-inch cock was damn big . . . thick, too.

Rawlins had urged Deckart to enjoy a soak in the jetted tub he'd admired so much their first day together. He'd added bath salts and oil, which he knew would soothe what had to be his lover's tender ass. Then Rawlins had given him his tablet, which had a reading app on it, and had helped him log into his own information.

After giving Deckart a deep kiss, Rawlins had winked and told him, "Relax for a bit. I'll be back shortly with a bottle of wine for you to enjoy." He'd paused in the doorway and asked, "You had a glass of Malbec the other day. Want that again?"

Seeing the way Deckart's eyes had lit up answered even before his mate's, "Yes, please."

When Rawlins had called the kitchen, Bobbi Jo had assured him that they would have a bottle brought right up. At the same time, he'd requested some finger food items that wouldn't be difficult to munch on in the tub — crackers, cheese slices in a variety of flavors, pepperoni chunks, ruffled chips with French onion dip, and carrot sticks with ranch dip. Considering Deckart had always been happy to eat whatever Rawlins had made over the last few days — frozen pizzas, frozen lasagna, baked fries and hot wings, pancakes, eggs in a variety of ways, plus hashbrowns and toast — he realized they really needed to have a conversation about food choices.

Hearing his doorbell ring, Rawlins hustled over. He opened it and found Bobbi Jo on the other side, a huge smile on her beaming features. "Hey, Rawlins," she greeted. "I heard you found your mate. He around for me to meet?" With Bobbi Jo speaking so enthusiastically, her southern accent was on clear display.

Rawlins shook his head. "Sorry, Bobbi Jo. He's taking a bath and relaxing." Pointing at the tray, he admitted, "This is to keep him fed while he does that."

Bobbi Jo hummed and smirked. "Ah, the joys of a new bond. I remember those days." She snickered, her brown eyes taking on a reminiscent gleam as she obviously remembered bonding with her tortoise mate. Then Bobbi Jo grinned at him again. "You take good care of him, sugar. It only gets better." With a suggestive eyebrow waggle, she turned away and waved good-bye.

Chuckling softly, Rawlins shook his head as he wheeled the trolley into the room. She and her husband — Darrell — had been bonded for over seventy years, and he knew they still acted like newlyweds. He prayed to any gods who cared to listen that he and Deckart would be that way, too.

After closing the door and locking it, Rawlins pushed the tray toward his bedroom. In there, he dropped his shorts and grabbed his *Kindle* device. He didn't plan to fuck Deckart in the tub, no matter how much fun that would be.

Another time.

No, this time was for cuddling, eating, reading, and talking.

Whatever my mate prefers.

"Hey, babe," Rawlins called softly as he headed into the bathroom. "I brought your wine and a few other things."

The sight of Deckart in the tub was damn provocative, but Rawlins refused to deviate his plans. "Let's start with the wine." He removed the temporary stopper the kitchen staff had placed in it, having already removed the normal one, and poured them both a glass. After taking a sip, finding it fresh and robust, Rawlins handed the other glass to Deckart. "Tell me what you think."

Deckart took a sip, then hummed, expressing his appreciation.

Rawlins smiled as he rolled the trolley to the side of the tub. "Here's a few snacks to enjoy while we're whiling away the evening." He locked the brakes so it wouldn't move before asking, "Do you mind sitting up a little so I can slip in behind you?"

Guess I should have asked first. What if he says no?

To Rawlins's relief, Deckart immediately scooted forward a little. There really was plenty of room. His smile and scent of pleasure also laid Rawlins's fears to rest.

Carefully, Rawlins climbed in behind Deckart. He slipped his legs on either side of the man and eased to a sitting position behind him. After relaxing back on the tub's curved backrest, Rawlins wrapped his left arm around Deckart's waist and tucked him close to his chest.

Rawlins nuzzled the back of Deckart's neck with his cheek while whispering, "This is fantastic. Love holding you, no matter the situation."

Deckart sighed and snuggled against him. "Definitely." Then he turned his head and pecked Rawlins's jaw before taking another sip of his wine. "So, what'd you bring?"

After Rawlins grabbed his wine glass and took a sip of his own, he put it down and began offering choices. "It's all finger foods," he assured. "Meat, cheese, crackers, chips and dip, carrots and dip. Simple but tasty."

After placing the tablet Rawlins had given him on another shelf of the trolley, Deckart stated with a chuckle, "And there's something from every food group. Salty, savory, and sweet." Then he picked up a saucer plate and began placing food on it.

Chuckling, Rawlins asked, "Okay, explain that."

Deckart glanced at him, a grin stretching his lips. "Salty." He pointed at the chips and crackers. "Savory." He indicated the meat and cheese. "Sweet." Deckart hummed as he scooped up a dollop of French onion dip.

Grinning, pleased to be providing for his mate, Rawlins nodded. "Got it." He watched Deckart swipe a baby carrot through the ranch before popping it into his mouth. Then he began making his own plate. "So, we never did actually talk about food preferences. Anything I should know? Favorites? Dislikes? Allergic to something?"

With a shrug, Deckart picked up a pepperoni cube. "I'm pretty easy to please. My family disowned me when I came out, so I had to make my own way in college." He popped it into his mouth, then mumbled around it, "*Ramen* noodles and me were best friends."

Wincing, Rawlins murmured, "I'm so sorry."

"Actually, even after all this time, I still like *Ramen* noodles." Deckart grinned as he claimed, "I happen to like salt, and considering it's a natural component to the human body, as long as you drink enough water to piss out the excess, I'm a firm believer that eating too much salt is a myth." Winking, Deckart added, "Plus, I read it in a book put out by a doctor about myths that have been perpetuated by misinformation."

"I've never really paid much attention," Rawlins admitted with a shrug. "A paranormal's metabolism is pretty damn fast, so we get the privilege of being able to eat and drink whatever we want." Setting his plate down, he reached into the water and palmed his bit of extra stomach flesh. "I had to come to grips with this a couple of centuries ago. My animal requires it. Best I can figure, it's due to being a mollusk and needing the insulation from cold water."

"Huh. Makes sense." Then Deckart scooped a chip through the French onion dip. "And I think you're sexy-as-fuck just the way you are."

Humming appreciatively, Rawlins dried his hand so he could grab a cube of cheese. Before popping it into his mouth, he frowned, recalling what else Deckart had said. "Uh, I was actually saying sorry for your family disowning you."

Deckart's eyes widened for a second before he snorted a laugh. With a roll of his eyes, he shook his head and stated, "Don't be." He waved between their bodies. "They were totally religious zealots of the fire and brimstone variety. There was very little love in that house." Deckart's brows furrowed as he mused, "I guess I feel the most bad for my little brother. He was only ten when they kicked me out nine years ago."

"I'm sure we could track him down if you're interested," Rawlins offered automatically, wanting his mate happy. "We have the resources."

"I'll think about it," Deckart responded, verbally brushing him off. Before Rawlins could press, his mate stated, "And I'm allergic to the oil on the skin of mangoes and zucchini. Can't touch the stuff, or I break out in hives."

Rawlins quickly nodded. "Got it. If we want to eat it, we'll have it prepared in the kitchen, or I'll do it myself."

54

Deckart smiled. "Thanks."

They continued eating and sharing, and Rawlins reveled in the easy camaraderie growing between them.

CHAPTER SEVEN

While Deckart looked forward to getting some more clothes . . . as well as a few other things . . . from his apartment, he didn't relish what he might face just to get into the building. Even though he knew he should have, Deckart hadn't admitted to Rawlins that every time he'd turned on his phone to make a call to his boss, he'd had several messages from Bart—ranging from belligerent to cajoling to scary.

What if he's waiting outside my apartment building?

"Are you okay, my mate?" Rawlins rumbled, squeezing the hand he held on the center console. "I can scent your unease. What's wrong?"

Knowing he had to come clean, Deckart admitted, "Bart's been leaving me messages."

Growling softly, Rawlins demanded, "What has that bastard been saying to you? You're mine, no matter what he's promising."

Gaping, Deckart snapped his attention to Rawlins. He saw the tight lines on his face, and for an instant, he thought he saw insecurity within the depths of his gray eyes. Shaking his head, Deckart couldn't believe his shifter could possibly feel insecure, but it was obvious that he was.

Deckart placed his free hand over their combined ones. "I'll never leave you," he declared. "I'm yours. Always."

Blowing out a breath, Rawlins glanced his way, his features twisting into a grimace for an instant. "Sorry, I—" He sighed again before admitting, "I could tell you were hiding something from me. I was worried."

The slow sensual loving Rawlins had bestowed upon Deckart the evening before suddenly made sense. His shifter had agreed to take him to his apartment so he could gather a few things. Maybe Rawlins had worried that, once Deckart returned home, he wouldn't want to go back to the marine park living arrangements again.

Nothing could have been further from the truth. If there weren't certain things that he really wanted to keep—a few personal mementos from childhood and college—he would have just written everything off. It wasn't as if his furniture was anything worth keeping.

"Well, Bart's just being a belligerent ass on the messages, but he's a big guy. A bodybuilder." Sighing, Deckart rubbed his wrist, even though the bruises were long gone. Having bonded with his shifter had sped up his healing, which was super nice. "His fists hit hard, and I don't want anything to happen to you or any of your friends."

Pisces, Westram, and his mate, Noah, were in the pick-up truck behind the SUV they traveled in. They'd hung out with all of them a number of times. Noah had been in an abusive relationship, too, before Westram had saved him. Although, from the tidbits the timid man had dropped, his situation had been far worse than Deckart's own.

"If anyone so much as looks cross-eyed at Noah, Westram will tear them apart," Rawlins assured, obviously reading his mind. "And the guys can take care of themselves. Trust me." Then he smiled and squeezed Deckart's hand. "And I'll take care of you and me."

Blowing out a deep breath, Deckart nodded. "Okay." He frowned out the window as he grumbled, "I don't know why Bart can't just get over himself and leave me alone."

At that moment, Rawlins rolled by Deckart's apartment building, looking for a parking spot. As if talk of him had conjured the jerk, Bart stood on the stoop, looking around. As it happened, Bart happened to glance in Deckart's direction and spotted him in Rawlins's vehicle.

"Oh, shit," Deckart hissed, watching Bart stare after them, even taking a couple of steps. "He's here."

"Relax, Deckart," Rawlins crooned, squeezing his hand again. "We're in the middle of the street. He can't do anything to you here." Then his voice lowered, and a growl entered his voice. "And if he tries, I'm here to stop him. Remember, shifters are stronger, bodybuilder or not."

Deckart took a few deep inhales and exhales as Rawlins expertly parked the SUV. By the time his lover turned off the vehicle's engine, he thought he had himself under control. He reached for the door handle, but Rawlins grabbed his hand, staying the action.

"Sit tight until I open the door for you," Rawlins ordered.

While Deckart's first instinct was to ask why, a glance in the side mirror gave him the answer. Bart was moving swiftly toward the SUV. His eyes were narrowed, and anger clouded the man's features.

"Y-Yeah. Okay."

Rawlins squeezed his hand once more in silent support before cracking his own door. He immediately locked the vehicle as he waited for it to be safe to exit on the side of traffic. Good thing he'd had the foresight to do that because before Rawlins managed to round the vehicle and get to Deckart's door, Bart was there trying to open it.

Bart frowned even further when it wouldn't budge. "Unlock the damn door, Deckart," he demanded, pulling on the handle once more.

Deckart could actually hear the metal groan with the force Bart was putting on it.

"Step away from my vehicle," Rawlins demanded as he stalked toward Bart and Deckart's door. "If you break it, I'll make certain you foot the bill."

Sneering at Rawlins, Bart looked him up and down with disdain in his eyes. "My boyfriend is in there," he stated, crossing his arms over his chest, accentuating his bulging pectorals. Deckart had always loved that feature about Bart, but now it just worried him. "If you don't open the door, I'm going to call the cops and tell them you're kidnapping him."

"Feel free to call the cops," Rawlins drawled, returning Bart's disdainful look. "It'll only get you into trouble." Waving toward the door, he moved closer while waving the key fob. "Back off so I can let my boyfriend out of my car."

"Your boyfriend?" Bart snapped incredulously. His face started to darken, blood rushing into his cheeks with his rising anger. "He ain't yours." Spittle gleamed on his thick lips as he all but screamed the words, "He's mine!"

Seeing the situation quickly unraveling, Deckart hastily unlocked the door and opened it. He slipped from the vehicle as swiftly as possible. Relief filled him when Rawlins stepped closer to him, forcing Bart to back up.

"You're not my boyfriend, Bart," Deckart declared softly, closing the SUV's door gently. "I broke up with you over two weeks ago." Shaking his head as he peered at the angry man, he added, "I don't know how much plainer I can say it."

"We both know you didn't mean it, Deck." Bart's voice took on a soothing tone, and he curved his features into a cajoling expression that used to make Deckart swoon. "You just caught me at a stressful moment. With all my training, it can happen sometimes." His laughter sounded a little strained as he tried to brush it off. "All that testosterone, ya know?"

Fortunately, after meeting a true gentle giant, Bart's words and actions had no effect on Deckart.

Or perhaps it's the mate-bond.

Deckart didn't know, and he didn't care. He just felt grateful. Easing closer to Rawlins, Deckart enjoyed the comfort that being close to his shifter brought him.

Unfortunately, Bart must have noticed the movement. His

eyes narrowed, and his face reddened once again. "Seriously?" he demanded. "You're cheating on me?"

Frustrated and tired of the whole damn thing, Deckart snapped, "It's hard to be cheating on you when we're not together. Leave me alone."

To Deckart's relief, Pisces, Westram, and Noah strolled up. While Westram kept his human mate close, Pisces inserted himself into the situation. He swept his gaze up and down Bart, and his expression declared that he wasn't impressed.

"This the abusive ex, Deckart?" Pisces asked.

Deckart fought back his groan. The usually happy-go-lucky guy was just tossing gas on the fire with those words. He could see it in the way Bart's eyes practically blazed with malice that he wanted to deck Pisces.

Only the arrival of a man in a cop's uniform stopped him.

"Hello, gentlemen," the dark-haired stranger greeted, sweeping his attention around the group. "Something wrong here?"

"Yeah," Bart started immediately, pointing at them. "These guys are holding my boyfriend against his will. They won't let Deckart away from them."

"Okay." The man took a few steps to the right, putting everyone to his left. Then he focused on Deckart and beckoned. "Can you come here please, sir?"

Glancing around, Deckart felt bile threaten his throat. He feared the cop actually believed Bart. He could barely believe it when Rawlins dipped his chin in a nod of encouragement.

Easing away from his shifter, Deckart moved to the cop's side. "I'm Officer Hastings," the guy told him. "Is there any truth to what that man said?" He tipped his chin in Bart's direction as he rested his hand on the butt of his service weapon. "Are you being held against your will?"

Relief filled him that Officer Hastings was actually trying to get to the bottom of things.

Deckart quickly shook his head. "No. That's Bart," he answered quietly, wanting to soothe the situation rather than inflame it. "He's my ex, but he's having trouble moving on. I have. Uh, moved on, I mean." Deckart flashed a smile in Rawlins's direction. "That's Rawlins, my new man. I really just want Bart to leave me alone so we can both get on with our lives."

"So that was him, huh?"

Rawlins overheard Noah's whispered words. The pair were in the bedroom packing.

Deckart's answer wasn't quite as quiet. "Yeah, that was him." He did sound tired, though, sad even.

"Well, at least your taste has improved this time around." Noah tried to come off as teasing, but it still sounded a little strained.

Fortunately, either Deckart didn't hear it, or he didn't want to draw attention to it. "That and gotta love the hand of Fate."

"How's Deckart holding up?" Pisces asked, much more discreetly. They were in the living room.

Deckart had told them that the only things he wanted were the books on his shelf that had a *From the Library of Deckart* label inside. They were cracking each one and checking before either putting it in the box or placing it back on the shelf.

"Okay, I think," Rawlins murmured back, picking up another book. "It helps that some random cop upheld his wishes, sending Bart on his way."

Westram snorted softly as he joined them. "Officer Baron Hastings wasn't so random." After another glance toward the door, he admitted, "After hearing about what was going on, I asked Grisham to see who'd be in the area and ask them to swing by around that time. Baron's a good guy from Grisham's precinct, or so he says."

Rawlins nodded slowly, processing that. Grisham was a police detective who was bonded with a small coconut octopus shifter. By all accounts, he was a good man and a better detective with fantastic instincts. Rawlins knew that the inner circle trusted his judgment, and he did, too, now.

Patting Rawlins on the back, Westram started back toward the kitchen where he'd been packing the food. "We take care of our own," he added softly before returning to his task.

Pisces snickered as he nodded. "Yep."

Rawlins had always known that, in theory. It wasn't until he'd needed help with his mate that he finally understood it in real life. His pod-members had his back, and by extension, they had Deckart's back, too.

With a smile on his face and relief in his heart, Rawlins went back to work.

Nearly three hours later, Rawlins's stomach rumbled aggressively. They'd finally finished loading everything Deckart wanted to keep in either Westram's pick-up truck or Rawlins's SUV. They were a little dirty, but their hunger was more important than getting cleaned up.

"Pizza parlor? Steakhouse? Chinese?" Westram asked.

They were trying to decide where to get food before returning to *World of Aquatica* housing.

"Oh, man." Deckart rubbed his stomach, and Rawlins heard his tummy talk, too. "All those sound amazing."

"Where's the nearest pizza place that makes good calzones?" Noah asked, perking up from where he'd been sprawled on the sofa, obviously tired. "I'd love a pepperoni and mushroom calzone right about now."

"Oh, me, too, baby," Westram returned eagerly. "And a three-meat pizza."

That caused Noah to bark a laugh, his green eyes dancing with mirth behind his gold-rimmed glasses.

Shifters had big appetites, after all.

"Hey, I'm down with a pizza joint," Pisces confirmed. He turned his attention to Deckart. "So? How about it? What's good around here?"

Deckart stared around at everyone like a deer in the headlights for a few seconds. Rawlins understood why they were singling out his mate. After all, he'd lived in the area for years, so he would know the best local haunts. Still, Rawlins had to fight back his desire to help out his mate, seeing as he looked so uncomfortable.

Fortunately, Deckart bounced back quickly. He grinned, declaring, "I know just the place. Their pies and calzones are the stuff of legends."

With anticipation in the air, they locked up Deckart's apartment, dropped off his notice at the superintendent's office, and headed out the door.

True to Deckart's word, the small mom-and-pop place tucked away on a side street truly outdid itself. The garlic knots they ordered as an appetizer were soft, flavorful, and had just the right amount of garlic. Their hot wing bites fell into the spicy just short of eye-watering category, which Rawlins loved.

With his tongue tingling, Rawlins bit deep into his slice of thin-crust three meat pizza. He was sharing the extra-large pie with Deckart, and they'd decided to add black olives, mushrooms, and on half of the pizza, jalapenos.

Yes, I'm a little bit of a spice nut.

Noah moaned as he ate a bite of his calzone, causing Westram to pin him with a heated expression. The other shifter didn't do anything other than fill his mouth with his meaty pizza, however. Still, any fool could see exactly what was going to happen between the pair when they arrived home.

As it should be.

Pisces relaxed in his chair, smirking at everyone. He leisurely ate his chicken alfredo pizza with a knife and fork. Occasionally, he enjoyed a bite of the bacon mac and cheese he'd spotted on the menu.

Rawlins appreciated that Pisces had offered everyone a bite because he intended to order a portion to go. He hoped to share it with his mate in lieu of dinner. After all, he couldn't imagine his mate wanting much after the feast they were enjoying.

As they headed out of the restaurant an hour and a half later, Rawlins felt certain he spotted Bart hanging out across the street. As they drove away, however, the annoying human disappeared in the crowds.

CHAPTER EIGHT

"Wow," Renaldo Martinez replied, his surprise clear, even through the phone line. "I can't say as I saw this coming." He chuckled before saying, "But I'm happy for you."

"Thanks." Deckart appreciated that his soon-to-be old boss was being so understanding. "And I really appreciate everything you did for me. I can't even"—he paused a second, getting his emotions under control—"I can't even tell you how much it means to me."

Renaldo scoffed softly. "I think I can imagine, but it was my pleasure." He paused before adding, "The right thing to do." Before Deckart could come up with a response, Renaldo snickered while saying, "So, I know how you can help me out. My daughter has wanted to go to *World of Aquatica* for over a year, ever since she read about their tiger shark show."

Deckart nodded even though he knew Renaldo couldn't see it. He knew how cool most people thought the show was. After all, no other marine park in the world had a show where tiger sharks leaped through hoops and lunged up for meat chunks. Deckart knew it was similar to some dolphin shows minus the riding on their backs.

In truth, the park could have incorporated that into the show. The tiger sharks in the show were actually shifters. Except, it would have been a little hard to explain.

"I bought tickets for her and her family, but the day they can go, the tiger shark show is already sold out." Renaldo sounded pained and frustrated. "I didn't realize I needed to buy them at the same time to be sure they could get in."

Humming, Deckart stated, "Yeah, it's one of their biggest attractions. You need tickets, right?" He wasn't going to make the man beg, not after how understanding he was being. Renaldo wasn't even making him return to work to finish out his two-week notice. "How many and what day?"

"God, do you really think you can get them?" Renaldo sounded so damn hopeful. It was a tone he'd never heard from the man. "If you can, I want to be there. I want to know what's so special about the damn show."

Deckart smirked, but he kept quiet. No way would he spill the beans about what was so special about the show.

"Uh, anyway, it's . . . Tuesday the fifth, and I need seats for five." Even though Deckart didn't need to know the information, Renaldo added, "My adult daughter, her husband, two kids under twelve, and myself."

"Got it," Deckart replied dutifully. "Three adults and two children. I can do that."

God, I sure hope I can do that.

I'll ask Rawlins. He'll know a way.

When Renaldo gushed his thanks for another five minutes, Deckart began to feel a little uncomfortable. Finally, the man wrapped it up by saying, "Well, I'll let you get back to enjoying your new man and learning the ropes of your new job."

Taking that opening, Deckart answered, "And I'll call you about those tickets soon."

"Thanks, Deckart," Renaldo replied. "You were one of our best. Keep in touch."

"I will, sir," Deckart answered on reflex, although he couldn't imagine why he would need to.

"Call me Renaldo, Deckart," the man corrected. "You're not my employee anymore."

After a second of hesitation, Deckart said, "Right. Renaldo. Talk to you soon."

"Thank you." Then Renaldo hung up.

As Deckart prepared to head to *World of Aquatica* in search of Rawlins, he didn't feel bad in the least that he'd misled his ex-boss. He'd told the man that he'd stumbled upon an old flame while on the beach—Rawlins. Rawlins worked at *World of Aquatica* and had secured him a job. The place was safe, with plenty of security, and he wouldn't have to worry about Bart.

Renaldo had said he understood—love and self-preservation were powerful motivators for change.

Hurrying out the apartment's door, Deckart shot off a quick text to Rawlins. *Where are you?* His lover and his people had secured him a new phone and phone number, allowing him to leave behind Bart and his pesky calls. He'd also wandered through the park several times with Rawlins, and he knew where most things were located.

Cleaning the glass on the Barrier Reef restaurant. You joining me for lunch in twenty? That was followed by a huge smiley emoji.

Deckart loved that Rawlins was always clearly happy to see him, and he didn't bother trying to stop his own grin. He never had to guess where he stood with his shifter. The man cared about him and never hid it.

I am. Deckart stepped into the elevator and hit the button for the main floor. *Just got off the phone with Renaldo. Need to talk to you about tiger shark show tickets.*

The bell dinged, indicating he'd reached his floor. After the door opened, he hurried out of the building. After climbing onto his *Vespa*, he turned the key, and it rumbled smoothly to life.

Impressed with the improvement, Deckart started on his way. His machine had never run so well. Evidently, the first thing fellow pod-member, Colton, did when a new member joined them, was check over their vehicle. The seahorse shifter was a master mechanic and always made certain everyone's rides were in top-notch condition.

On the plus side of Deckart's particular ride, his *Vespa* fit on the golf cart road that led from *World of Aquatica*'s lodging buildings to the park proper. He never had to leave the secured area. Deckart felt safe, knowing he was never leaving shifter property.

Arriving at the edge of the park, Deckart parked his scooter off to the side. While he could drive it *to* the park, he couldn't drive it *around* the park. That would have been beyond rude unless it was an emergency.

Visiting his man wasn't an emergency.

Too bad.

After leaving his ride behind, Deckart began strolling through the park. He knew he was a few minutes early, but that was okay. He could sit and read while waiting for Rawlins to finish. Deckart just really wanted to be with his mate.

Weird shifter mate-bond shit.

Deckart smiled at the thought. He didn't mind.

With his head in the clouds, Deckart wasn't paying attention to those around him. A strong arm around his torso and someone yanking him into the alley changed that quick, fast, and in a hurry.

Too bad when he heard someone whisper harshly into his ear, "Told you we weren't done," a voice he recognized as Bart's, there wasn't a damn thing he could do about it.

"Hey, Rawlins," Eban rumbled, drawing his attention to the approaching head enforcer. "You expecting your man for lunch?"

"Yeah," Rawlins confirmed, grinning broadly. Then he glanced at the time displayed on his phone and frowned. "In fact, he should have been here by now."

Before Rawlins could pull up Deckart's number, Eban gripped his wrist. "That's what I thought. You need to see this."

Frowning, Rawlins followed docilely when Eban tugged him between buildings and into the shade. Then the man pulled out a tablet and punched a few buttons. He grimaced once, then tapped at it again.

Rawlins wanted to tell Eban to hurry the fuck up, but a shifter didn't say that sort of thing to their pod's head enforcer.

Finally, Eban held out the device and ordered, "Watch."

Obeying, Rawlins watched his mate appear within the camera view. He smiled upon seeing the clearly relaxed expression on his lover's face. Just as quickly, he snarled, rage surging through him as he watched Bart slip from an alley Deckart had just passed, grab him around the torso, clap a hand over his mouth, and drag him backward and out of view.

"Where are they?" Rawlins demanded, focusing on Eban. "How long ago did this happen?"

To Rawlins's surprise, Eban smirked at him. "That was ten minutes ago. The dumbass took Deckart to the back area of the sunken ship exhibit." With a roll of his eyes, he beckoned for his tablet back. "Don't worry. He won't get far. We care for our own."

Rawlins growled as he handed back the tablet. He wanted to run, but he knew that wasn't wise. After all, he would be going in blind. Rawlins needed Eban to give him a visual, and from how he was tapping on the screen, he figured the head enforcer was doing just that.

"So, here's real-time." Eban passed over the tablet again. "From six cameras. It looks like he's on the south side." Snorting, he added, "Aaand, he's already caught the attention of several shifters in the aquarium." Eban chuckled, smirking as he ordered, "Just keep watching. Your man will be safe soon enough."

Even as Rawlins focused on the screen, Eban grabbed his upper arm and sped up their stride. "Keep up and keep watching," he ordered. "I know you won't be able to concentrate enough to do both."

Eban was right because as soon as Rawlins spotted Deckart sitting at Bart's feet on the metal walkway that crisscrossed around and over the massive network of aquariums, he couldn't tear his gaze away from the screen. He couldn't tell what Bart was saying, only that he was yelling something at Deckart. His face was once again red with his anger, and his biceps bulged as if he were flexing them threateningly.

Gods, what an asshole. If I get my hands on him, I'm going to —

Evidently, Eban was managing to pay attention to not only where they were going but to what was happening on the screens, too. "Oh, look at that. Darrell just gave a head-bob to Kenny." He snickered cruelly, referring to Darrell's massive sea tortoise, as he muttered, "That won't be good for Bart."

Rawlins winced just at the thoughts that conjured. Kenny was a sea snake shifter. His kind were known as coral reef snakes, the coral snake of the sea. He had enough venom in his bite to take down a large shifter, should he decide to utilize everything in his venom sacks.

When Rawlins saw Kenny's milky-white and black banded body appear on screen, he sucked in a sharp breath. The snake shifter cut through the water lightning-fast, moving one way, then the other, underneath the scaffolding. While a traditional sea snake couldn't move well, if at all, on dry land due to their aquatic nature, Rawlins would guess that Kenny didn't have that problem.

After all, Kenny was a shifter who could reason and think.

Evidently, whatever Bart had been yelling — maybe threatening — urged Kenny to act. The snake shifter streaked through the water and shot up between the metal slats. He sank his fangs into Bart's calf, causing the human to scream and jump.

Just as quickly, Kenny released him. He slithered off the side of the metal scaffolding and plopped back into the water. The shifter didn't go far, moving back and forth near Darrell's much larger, shelled body.

Bart crumpled onto his butt, grabbing his leg while peering fearfully at the water below him, and Deckart took the opportunity to crab-walk backward, putting plenty of space between them.

"Stop staring and get in there, Rawlins," Eban snapped, yanking him out of his focus of the screen.

Rawlins realized they'd made it to a side entrance to the employee's only area of the exhibit. His mate was just a little way inside. Shoving the tablet at Eban, Rawlins rushed inside. He glanced around, then began sprinting to the left.

He'd cleaned the aquariums' walls—inside and out—more times than he could count, and he knew exactly where Deckart was. Calling his mate's name, he sprinted up a set of stairs, along a walkway, then to another set of stairs. He spotted Deckart curled up at the top and took them three at a time.

Once Rawlins reached Deckart, he swept his mate into his arms and clutched him close. "Are you okay?" he hissed into his ear, nuzzling his neck. "Did he hurt you?"

"I'm okay," Deckart assured, rubbing up and down Rawlins's back, soothing him. "I'm okay." Then he turned his head and looked toward Bart. "But Bart was bitten by something."

"I know," Rawlins whispered. "He was bitten by Kenny. I don't know what Bart was raving about. I couldn't hear him, but Kenny must have thought a fellow shifter's mate was in danger." Rawlins peered in the snake's direction and smiled. "Thanks, man."

"Oh." Deckart looked that way, too. "He's a shifter, too." He settled and relaxed. "Okay."

"What are you talking about?" Bart cried, glancing around

71

while rocking a bit. "Come on, guys. Call an ambulance." Rawlins could actually hear the pain and fear in the man's voice. "That snake bit me, and whatever shit it has in its poison burns." Then Bart glared at Deckart. "This is all your fault, you slutty bitch. If you'd known your place, I wouldn't be in this mess."

Before Rawlins could give in to his urge to cross to the man and toss him into the aquarium for the real sharks to finish off, Kaiser stepped from the shadows at the other end of the latticework. "You know, it would be such a fitting end for an asshole like you to die from a snake bite." Kaiser sauntered forward, followed by Doctor Anthony Keller. "A cautionary tale, if you will. A man breaks into a marine park to kidnap his ex-boyfriend, only to be bitten and killed by one of the animals when he tries to run away through a secured area." His deep green eyes glittered with malice as he stared down at a pained and fear-filled Bart. "I know I could spin it that way to the press. They love a salacious story."

Bart whimpered, the sound at odds with his massive frame.

Kaiser continued to stare at him coldly for several heartbeats before he curled his lip in obvious disgust. "But the paperwork and interviews and inspections would be a waste of my time." Waving his hand, he ordered, "Doc. The antivenom?"

Anthony opened his bag as he strode forward. "I suppose. Such a waste to be used on this man." As he prepped a syringe, he added, "You know, Kenny doesn't appreciate going through the milking process needed to make the anti-venom any more than I do."

Scoffing, Kaiser nodded. "I know, but he also understands why it must be done." Then he turned his attention to the sea snake wriggling back and forth in the water nearby. "And don't worry. Price is on his way. He's going to make Bart forgets all about Deckart."

"I will?" Price strode into view, glancing around at everyone. "All memories or just some?"

"*All* memories of Deckart," Kaiser confirmed. Then his smile turned predatory as he focused on Price. "And if you don't mind, make him a little . . . *nicer*." He sneered at Bart. "No more bullying ways."

Price nodded once. "You got it." Then his eyes hazed, the ice-blue of his irises bleeding to red.

Bart whimpered once before his feature went slack, the vampire obviously doing exactly as their alpha had requested.

Kaiser's features softened as he turned his attention on Rawlins and Deckart. "Are you okay, Deckart? Does the doc need to check you over?"

Deckart shook his head, never moving from the safety of Rawlins's embrace. "No, thanks, Kaiser," he murmured with a smile. "Bart didn't have time to hurt me. You all stopped him first." Cuddling even closer, Deckart added, "Thank you." His attention lowered to the snake in the water. "And thanks to you, Kenny."

"You're welcome, Deckart," Kaiser replied. "You're one of ours. We'll always protect you." Then he frowned at Eban. "Do a sweep. Figure out how this asshole got in here. I know everyone was notified of what he looked like."

Eban nodded. "Yes, Alpha. We'll figure it out."

Kaiser grunted. "See that you do." Then he returned his attention to Rawlins. "Why don't you take the rest of the day off, Rawlins," he encouraged. "See to your mate. I know you need it."

"Thank you, Alpha," Rawlins replied, relief flooding him that he wouldn't have to fight his protective nature by going back to work. "I appreciate it."

"Of course," Kaiser replied.

As Rawlins led his still unsteady Deckart down the stairs, he heard his alpha call, "And the windows of *Mini Barrier Reef Cantina* have never looked better, Rawlins. Glad to have you back at work."

Rawlins grinned, chuckled even, before he decided to just lift his willing mate into his arms and sprint away. Intent on checking every inch of his mate for . . . everything . . . just because he could, he almost smiled as he looked forward to sharing one of Deckart's favorite things with him . . . their tub.

And it won't just be my pleasure.

ABOUT THE AUTHOR

Charlie started writing fantasy when she was eight, and after stumbling onto her first erotic romance at age nineteen, she realized her true calling. She now focuses on writing gay erotic romance, normally of the paranormal variety, with heroes of all kinds. With the help and support of her husband, Charlie finally fulfilled one of her life-long goals . . . move to acreage with her horses. You can often find her curled up with her laptop and a cup of tea or glass of wine, creating her next adventure. Charlie enjoys exploring the mountains of her new Oregon home on horseback, 4-wheeler, or motorcycle.

She can be reached at ch.richards2010@yahoo.com
Or visit her at www.charlie-richards.com.